SKYE CI[...]
THE SKELETONS O[...]
EPISODE C[...]
THE TRANSHUMAN REVOLUTION

Written by R. D. Hale

Copyright © 2010, 2018 by R. D. Hale

Laniakea Publishing

ALL RIGHTS RESERVED. This book contains material protected under international laws and treaties. Any unauthorised reprint or use of this material is prohibited. No part of this book may be reproduced or transmitted in any form or by any means, electronic or mechanical, including photocopying, recording, or by any information storage and retrieval system without written permission from the author.

PRAISE FOR R. D. HALE:

'A wonderfully written piece that goes beyond the action and excitement of overcoming a corrupt social system and digs deeper: rising from the ashes of despair.' **D. L. Denham - Red Denver**

'I think readers will look back on this in a few years and boast "I remember discovering his first book and telling my friends..."' **Dale L. Sproule - Psychedelia Gothique**

'The narration is a character itself as R.D Hale's true talent is with building a world with words and paint a picture for the reader with full on assault of the English language.' **David J. Thirteen - Mr. 8**

'The characters are engaging, the plot is interesting, the dialogue is witty, the action is entertaining, and the fictional world is quite spectacular.' **Cameron W. Kobes - Tales of Cynings**

'This book interweaves heavy social issues and philosophy, milking the sci-fi genre for all its worth. The slumdogs' efforts to maintain their humanity in such a heartless age, when everything is going against them is palpable. The 99% versus 1% theme focuses our minds on where society might be heading and forces us to look at things how they are, if we wish them to be truly different.' **Dean C. Moore - Author of Renaissance 2.0**

FOREWORD

R. D. Hale really does not know when to stop. I mean, he has only gone and written a prequel now. This one even more morally bankrupt and substandard than the rest of the series, mainly thanks to the change of protagonist. You will now be viewing Eryx through the eyes of the manipulative and ruthless Leo Jardine, back in his younger days.

Alas, I have been tasked with introducing you to this nonsense so please do not blame me when it lets you down. I tried my best to warn you. I am assuming you have read Hale's other works in which case I must ask, what type of weirdo are you?

Just go ahead and read The Transhuman Revolution if you must. If you are really patient, try and persevere until the end, through the desperation, the unholy bloodshed, the lies and deceit, the substance abuse, the criminality, the treachery. Did I mention the bloodshed?

Should you choose to visit the year 2030, you will probably be scarred, and certainly stunned, by the process, but you will have achieved something, survived an ordeal, a trial. And you will gain a masterclass in how not to be a human (as well as how not to write).

To be fair, Hale has been through a lot, begging the question of whether he can really be held responsible for this crap. And now he has a third child on the way. As if he did not have enough grey hairs already. Writing has become his full time occupation, meaning he has no escape from the pains of daily life and is solely dependent on a profession in which he has no talent. None. Zero. Zilch.

And to top it all off, his main rival for the title of world's biggest idiot has only gone and won the US Presidency. Fucking wonderful.

GLOSSARY

Compuscreen (CUS) – a computer composed of two perpendicular touchscreens.
Holoscreen – a flat-screen computer which creates a pseudo three-dimensional image.
Projector – a computer which projects photorealistic holograms of any size.
Holowatch – a mini-projector which wraps around the wrist.
Citicard – the identification card used by Citizens which acts as a debit card and access pass.
Phaser – a generic term for small weapons which fire plasma pulses or energy beams.
Rail Gun – high-powered rifles which fire bullets via an electro-magnetic charge.
Rubbish Deposit System (RDS) – transports rubbish to landfill via conduits which provide useful escape routes for those fleeing the law.
Delos Pod – a two-person pod capable of flying at only ten miles an hour.
Maglev Car – a vehicle which uses magnetic hovering technology on maglev highways, but reverts to wheels when offroad.
Samarianism – the dominant religion of Anatolia.
Samaris – the saviour of the Samarian religion.
Goddess Katona – the deity worshipped by Samarians.
The Underlord – an alternative name for the Devil in Samarianism.
The Elites – a name for the political leaders and clergy of Anatolia.
San Teria – the theocratic ruling party of Anatolia.
San Terian Guard – the police force of Anatolia.
Elite Guard – Anatolia's equivalent of a special weapons and tactics (SWAT) team.
Medio – the capital city of Anatolia with a population of over thirty million.
Underworld – a town which was once an underground train system and mall, but is now home to criminals. (Named after the Samarian version of Hell.)
Old town – the name given to derelict areas of Medio which have since been overtaken by criminals and bottom-levellers.
Inner-hub – an area of Medio reserved for Level One and Two Citizens which cannot be accessed without a Citicard.
Outer-hub – an area of Medio mainly reserved for Citizens. Most buildings cannot be accessed without a Citicard.

The Hanging Gardens – a number of islands floating above Medio which can only be accessed with a Level One Citicard.

Mukat – a historical town of religious importance.

Skye City – three towers with three adjoining plateaus at the heart of Medio, standing over two miles tall.

Sky Elevator – joins the central tower of Skye City to Orbital City.

Orbital City – a space station which is the control centre of the Planet Eryx.

Anatolia – the last remaining superpower on planet Eryx.

Nyberu – the other super-power on Eryx which was left in ruins after The Great War.

Planet Eryx – the third of a nine planet system orbiting a red dwarf.

Taranath – the largest of Anatolia's two moons.

Mani – the smallest of Anatolia's two moons.

Level One Citizens – the wealthiest members of Anatolian society. Many have upgraded their bodies with cybernetic and genetic modifications.

Level Two Citizens – these people are able to live comfortably, but denied the great luxury of Level One Citizenship.

Level Three Citizens – these people live impoverished lives and work long hours in poor conditions.

Bottom-levellers – outcasts who have refused to accept Level Three Citizenship and have few legal rights.

The Rebellion – a group of outlaws who have joined forces with foreign armies to overthrow San Teria.

Mutants – a generic term to describe creatures created through genetic engineering or radioactive mutation.

Telepaths – genetically-engineered humans with various paranormal abilities.

Hoverbots – small hovering robots, some of which fire webs of glue to ensnare criminals.

Mechanoids – large, powerful robots used in industry and combat.

Androids – human-like robots used as servants, especially in retail and other service industries.

SKYE CITY

THE SKELETONS OF JARDINE

EPISODE ONE

THE TRANSHUMAN REVOLUTION

'No, if destruction be our lot we must ourselves be its author and finisher. As a nation of free men we will live forever or die by suicide.'
Abraham Lincoln

Disaster

WAVES CRASH ONTO THE DECK of this patched-up frigate, making it impossible to maintain a foothold without the aid of the handrail. The frigate rocks and I fall halfway to my backside, almost dislocating my shoulder as one hand grips slippery metal tight. Pulling this mass of steroid-enhanced flab back to my feet, I stare at jagged black clouds against a tinge of redness; a sky of semi-molten lava agitating the miserable, grey ocean.

It is a nightmare, an endless void waiting to swallow those who venture where they do not belong. And the near-constant sight of cabin boys spewing, only adds to the misery of this pointless campaign.

'Haul your arse over here, you clumsy bastard,' Anguson roars over the thunder of forty thousand fathoms of tempestuousness determined to add another wreck to the world's largest and wettest graveyard. Shaking my head and clenching my teeth, I haul myself along the cabin wall for the twentieth bastard time. I swear they will force me to keep doing this until I go ov… BANG!

A scorching wind smashes me against the side-railing; the shockwave crippling my vertebrae. I hook my numbed arm through a rusted bar to stop this useless lump of meat being tossed overboard. Clinging on until salty air refills my lungs, I swing my head around and glimpse flames consuming the shards of broken decking. The crippled frigate tilts and if I lose my grip, I will slide down this sloping surface, joining my shipmates in fire.

'Jardine, this thing's going down. Get to the fucking lifeboat, now!' Anguson roars as he sticks a leg into one of the orange orbs on which our worthless lives now depend.

With no better option, I let go of the railing and wave my arms in an attempt to steer towards the lifeboat, but the frigate lurches steeper and I am somersaulted, clattering into something hard. The pain in my head is agonising, overwhelming my other senses as I tumble ever faster… and SPLASH! Vision blurs as turbulent H2O surrounds my sinking, motionless body.

Brine invades my nostrils and after several agonising attempts at breathing, a genius thought occurs – hold my damn breath. If I do not start swimming soon I will be fish food, but my enfeebled limbs squirm without co-ordination, and I have no clue which way is up or down.

Images are smeared by salt water, the faces of men, apparently dead, or at the very least, hideously disfigured. One drifts towards mine and greenish features sharpen until it resembles my late father; his swirling beard, broad nose, and angular eye-folds unmistakable, even in the turbulence. 'Swim up!' he yells in a garbled tone, pointing to the surface, then my hero vanishes, dissolving into bloodiness.

Somehow I tear off my leather boots without undoing the laces and then I flail my fat, clumsy limbs. The effort of 'swimming' fills my lungs and eyeballs with agony until they are ready to burst. Do. Not. Breathe. I kick my legs. And kick. And kick. And release… My short beard breaches the surface; neck twisting, head jerking for signs of help.

Bobbing in the waves, I gasp and spit as lightning reveals an orange orb - a solitary beacon of hope. I wave to this lifeboat as though it has fucking eyes, but a wave smashes my head underwater like the fist of the Nyberun Sea God.

I swallow brine. Cough. Flail again. Breach the surface again. Gasp again. Spit again.

'Over here!' I roar, waving my arms, swimming clumsily, plunging underwater, breaching the surface, swimming, gasping, spitting. Breathing almost impossible, progress limited, the orange orb too far. CRASH! Darkness…

Slap… Slap… Cheeks sting. Voices are muffled. 'Ickop olbadart. Wickup olf badard. Wake up, you stupid old bastard, I have no desire to perform mouth to mouth on you!'

I cough bloody brine and wheeze as daggers are torn from my man-tits, or so it feels. The cage-hardened eyes of Sydney Anguson stare as I process what my rescuer just said. 'Mouth to mouth… w-would achieve nothing… other than turn you on.' I laugh, sitting up on slippery plastic to see Bilton, one of the cabin boys, swaying in the confines of the shadowy orb. And no-one else.

'My skill is hurting people, not saving them. Most went down with the ship. You're the only one we could find. Bloody Nyberun rocket took us down.'

'And now I'm stuck with you two in the middle of the Panthalassic Ocean. Something tells me this is going to be a miserable experience.'

ADRIFT

For days we drift; light sporadically breaching the orange walls of our lifeboat like we are enclosed within a dying sun. My shipmates become near-invisible during phases of darkness which seem everlasting. The aggression of the Panthalassic Ocean makes sleep impossible and the temperature is always too high or low.

The seats are organised in four rows of ten, two either side of a walkway, or rather crawlway, facing inwards. Leaving your seat means getting tossed around, staying strapped in means unbearable restlessness. Our leaders did not supply our lifeboats with food, water, or communications equipment, and will not be in a hurry to rescue three expendables likely presumed dead. We are effectively fucked.

Bilton, the cabin boy, barely speaks, just clings to the straps of his seat. Tears are revealed whenever the ocean lifts his low gaze. Anguson never shuts his trap and the temptation to throw the cage-fighter overboard is strong, not that I could.

'I swear I've lost about thirty pounds,' I say during a period of orange-tinged light as my stomach is twisted by the pain of hunger.

'Well, you needed to lose weight,' Anguson booms with an unfathomable burst of energy. 'Could be the best thing that ever happened to him, eh Bilton?' The cabin boy remains muted, but his lips move a little, mouthing: *Yeah*. Cheeky shit.

'Best thing? Men have died, not that I was attached to them, but we should at least respect their memory. Two years fighting someone else's war together, that's a long time,' I say.

'Two years on the wrong fucking side.' Anguson growls. 'No more of this shit. When we make it back, I won't be fighting for those bastards again. I'm a fucking celebrity. How the hell can a superstar athlete be conscripted? Ridiculous.'

'Not sure if *athlete* is the right word, Anguson, you're a steroid-enhanced cock-fighter.' I laugh in pathetic, soundless gasps.

'Steroids? Cheeky bastard,' Anguson says.

Bumping into Bilton's shins, I crawl to the doorway and unzip both sets of flaps. As I grip a fabric handle on the wall, the cold seawater splashes my face. Invigorating. I rub my eyelids, seeing nothing but waves reflecting the pink sky – a sky tainted by anti-matter weapons turning the most populous areas of Nyberu to dust. *A necessary evil,* San Teria says.

'Can't be long till landfall, surely?' Anguson mutters.

'Depends how you define *long*. The ocean's about twelve thousand miles across, but I'm guessing we're closer to Nyberu than Anatolia. Maybe a couple of thousand miles from irradiated desert, that's not far.'

'In that case, I need to decide which one of you I'm gonna eat first.' Anguson chuckles in a sinister tone and we know his choice if it comes to *that*. Not that a skinny cabin boy would make much of a meal.

Bilton wraps his arms around his shins, trembling slightly as he stares at the bearded cage-fighter. 'I just want to see her, my sister, she's all I have.' Bilton's acne-ridden face drops to hide his tears as his trembling becomes pronounced. And I want to offer words of encouragement, but I lack the energy to lie.

'Life's cruel, doesn't give a fuck who it hurts. Kids, celebrities, wretches like me, we're all the same,' I murmur.

'Yup, we can be taken in an instant, no matter what we have. We remain in denial until the moment arrives. I never expected to be stranded at sea, dying a slow and miserable death from thirst and starvation, though,' Anguson says and I look to Bilton whose face has become petrified; his flesh almost quite literally stone. He is not so much as blinking.

Many days pass with no sight of landfall. Bilton is growing a beard of sorts – thin, blonde, patchy – it only adds to his emaciated appearance. The hunger and thirst are so intense even Anguson has stopped making wisecracks – a couple of mouthfuls of rain is all we have drunk.

Food and water are all I can think about, talk about, dream about. For hours I hold my hand out of the unzipped door, praying for more rain. *Praying*. The fucking irony. I have not been so thin since I was a boy running through the slums of Medio city, but I am still fatter than most 'bottom-levellers'.

The cabin boy was already skinny but now he seems close to death. Giving up on his strapped seat, he rolls and groans; occasionally his eyelids open to confirm consciousness, other times he calls: *'Mary'*. Bile sloshes around the lifeboat from bouts of seasickness. Our clothes smell of *that*, saltwater, and stale sweat.

Lying awake on the crawlway with my eyes closed, I feel a nudge and turn to see a broad shadow so I sit upright and scratch my sticky head.

'You know we're dying, right? Mouthfuls of rainwater can't sustain us.' Anguson pauses as though waiting for me to suggest the unthinkable, but I refuse to make murder that easy. Anguson continues to whisper with a distinct sense of nervousness and shame: 'I reckon the kid has a couple of days at best. The more we deteriorate, the less chance we have. We need food now. Better that two of us make it.'

'What are you suggesting?' I croak as the outline of a sheath-knife confirms my suspicion, and I understand Anguson's logic. We are weak, withering, desperate.

'You mean, the boy? We ca…' Halfway through my sentence I lose the will to further object. Anguson shuffles towards the sleeping Bilton, and my hunger and conscience, body and soul, nullify one another in a tug of war.

My arm hairs are raised by a squelch, a splutter, a wheeze, a crunch, silence. I wince until my face muscles ache then hold my breath and bite my lips. Tears pour from my eyes as I shiver, feeling guilty, yet relieved. Food. Thanks to the Rule of the Sea.

'I'm sorry, kid, if there was another way…'

My broad, rigid back is turned, yellow teeth clenched, hairy lips curled – a disgusting monster listening to squelches of flesh and the cracking of bones. The other monster taps my shoulder. I flinch and then hold out my shivering palm with eyes closed, inhaling the smell of blood.

Something warm and soft slops onto my hand, then finds its way into my mouth which my fingers barely escape intact. I swallow the unspecified body part after one eye-watering chew and hold out my bloody hand for seconds. A few squelches later another lump slops into my palm, maybe Bilton's heart. The process repeats until my belly is full and I can feel my body being replenished second by second, calorie by calorie. Relief. Sickening relief.

Slowly, I turn to face Bilton's abdomen which is carved open like the cabin boy is undergoing a post-mortem examination, but darkness lessens the grisly details. Emotions are intense yet dulled, as though conflicting instincts have succeeded in neutralising any neurological response, other than a cannibal's urge to eat. I know guilt is buried in there somewhere.

'What should we do, Anguson? Throw him overboard? Give him a burial at sea? That would be the right thing to do,' I suggest, my voice barely more than a whisper.

'*This* is no longer a *he,* it's our only source of food, Jardine. Our one chance of survival. There's no way it's going overboard.'

For three days, we share the company of a shrinking human carcass until it seems no grimmer than a buffalo to a lion, in spite of the putrid smell. Upon waking, I commence my ritual of unzipping the door flaps and peering across the globe-spanning Panthalassic Ocean. The weather is calm with minimal waves bearing tiny diamonds below the blinding sun. I can see a fuzzy unevenness on the horizon, maybe a mirage, but still I tremble with hope.

'Anguson, take a look. I think…'

Anguson scrambles down the crawlway, almost barging me into the sea in his eagerness to look out the lifeboat door. Grasping the other handle, he places his hand over brow and laughs in long, wheezing breaths as we stand shoulder-to-shoulder, bobbing in tandem.

'Looks like land. Better hope we drift towards, rather than past it. Still too far to swim,' Anguson says.

'It fills the entire horizon; there's a tinge of green,' I say as the peak of a wave provides a better vantage. 'Looks way too big to be an island. Must be the Nyberun shoreline. We were closer than I thought.'

'Never thought I'd be so happy to see enemy territory,' Anguson says.

The orange orb drifts for what seems like a week, but there is no day-to-night cycle during this period in which the Nyberun coast gets incrementally closer. Every second we stare at luminous palms and a ribbon of sand, asking whether we are within swimming distance, but with our bulk I doubt we could swim more than one hundred yards.

'Hey, Jardine, what we gonna do when we reach land? The Nyberuns will likely skin us alive.'

'I've absolutely no idea. We're on the wrong side of the world with only the Panthalassic Ocean separating us from home. I doubt there's any way back until the war's over. I hope you remembered your survival training,' I say.

'We're getting closer. Ya think we should swim? Let's–'

'No, we'll need shelter when we reach land. The lifeboat can provide that,' I say.

'And it means we get to keep the food…'

Dry Land

WARM BREEZE IN MY FACE, I watch a beautiful, glorious beach coming so close I can no longer restrain my desire to reach dry land. The luminosity of palms seems supernatural as I jump from the lifeboat, relieved my bare feet meet the seabed in neck-deep water. Anguson does the same and we hold our chins aloft as we drag the orb by door-flaps towards golden grains; transitioning from Hell to Heaven. Two places I never believed in.

The sea becomes knee-deep, turquoise, transparent, unlike the brown sludge of Anatolia, and I laugh giddily until my foot meets a sharp pebble. 'Ow.' Anguson and I drag the lifeboat ashore, crossing hot sand on which the orb is so much heavier, and leaving it within palm trees where it should be less visible to passing vessels. And then I collapse onto cooler, shaded sand. Soft, white, perfect.

'We made it. We actually fucking made it.' I sigh.

'What next?' Anguson sits alongside me with arms around knees; his wet khaki uniform gleaming in sunlight which is streaking through the palms.

'Food... Drink... Coconuts would be the perfect start. Time to get climbing.' I laugh feebly, joyously.

'Are you fucking kidding me? The condition I'm in...'

'You're the one who keeps bragging about being a professional athlete. Time to prove it, tough guy.'

And with that, Anguson approaches a palm over two-storeys high; its leaves forming a black umbrella against the pink sky. The cage-fighter wraps his arms, legs and boots around the slender trunk and shuffles upwards, then slides to the ground. Anguson repeats the process, grunting and growling with each failed attempt; his sweaty face turning purple and his no-longer-huge biceps bulging.

'It's no use. My clothes are too wet.'

'It's true what they say – gorillas aren't great climbers,' I remark and Anguson sniffs sharply. 'The palm tree is tilted, meaning if you wrap your hands around, you can actually walk up. I've seen people do it on a documentary.'

'You're seriously telling me to walk up a palm tree?' Anguson raises his eyebrows which are gathering droplets of sweat.

'Yes, it's easy.' I place my hands behind my head, smiling as I lie on the sand, waiting for the 'world's greatest cage fighter' to do his thing, but he stands with hands on hips; an imposing silhouette looming over my face.

'In that case, let's see you do it.'

Sighing, I rise from the beach and approach the palm tree, locking my hands around the trunk. I place a sandy foot on the rough, grey bark, and then I walk upwards with minimal slippage. My flabby body is nimbler than I thought.

'See, I told you it's easy,' I yell, but then my body swings around so that I am dangling from the underside of the trunk. My hands slip and I plummet, landing on my back, unable to breathe as my chest muscles tighten. Good job the beach provided a soft landing.

Anguson bends over, pointing and wheezing with laughter as I sit up and curl my lips. A sunbeam burns my eyes as I turn towards the smart-arse.

'I made a better attempt than you... Okay, time for plan B,' I say.

'What's plan B?' Anguson says.

'We shake the palm tree until the coconuts fall,' I say.

'But won't that be painful – coconuts falling on our heads?' Anguson says.

'You've been struck by the toughest men on the planet and you're worried about a few lousy coconuts? Look at the top of the tree – the tilt of the trunk causes it to extend outwards. The coconuts should fall down *there*.'

We push and pull a coconut tree, but our pathetic efforts barely cause the green bunches to move, and we lack the strength to shake all day. 'This one's too big and strong. Let's look for a smaller, skinnier tree that we might have more luck with,' I say and we patrol the mesh of shadows on the coastline, but every coconut tree seems bigger than the last – some two, three times the height of a house. Staring at black and green fronds, I identify a 'sapling' which stands eight or nine yards tall.

'This one will have to do,' I gasp, and we shake the skinnier and less stubborn trunk which scrapes the skin from my hands. Two stranded idiots grunt and shake and grunt and shake, and I look to the thrashing leaves to see coconuts raining down. I leap out the way as a coconut cracks Anguson's skull and he plunges to the ground; blood seeping into his wild, greasy hair as he squirms.

'Shit, are you okay?' I say.

'I haven't been hit that hard since I fought Mickey 'The Beast' Malarkey in twenty-seven.' Anguson rubs his head and stares at the blood on his hand. 'We've got three coconuts. What now?'

'We open them, genius.' I collect two smooth, green coconuts – at least I hope they are coconuts – and I smash their protective husks together. Nothing. I smash again and again; the force of each impact jarring my arm-bones. 'Stubborn bastards won't open.'

'Here, let me try, you soft shite.'

Anguson collects the coconuts from my grasp and smashes the green husks together with a deafening roar. Still nothing. Tattooed fingers turn red and white under the strain of each effort and yet the coconut husks are unblemished. What the hell are they made of?

'I've got it – rocks. Let's find some rocks and smash the shit out of these bastards,' I suggest.

Anguson and I march along the curving beach until black rocks breach the turquoise waves and white foam. 'Longest damn beach in the world,' Anguson mutters as I splash through anemone-filled pools, approaching a jagged boulder.

Raising my hands above my head, I smash the coconut onto a sharp corner, and its green husk splits. I bash again and again, but the husk is spongy and fibrous, and will not just break in half. I tear out the fibres and attempt to prise the husk open, but the damn thing is bloody strong. I bash the other side, and bash, and gasp, and bash, creating another split, and then I just go (coco)nuts, bashing every part of the husk until multiple splits join. I tear the bastard apart to reveal my brown, hairy prize.

I bash the coconut shell on the rock. Nothing. Kill me.

'I swear to the fucking Goddess, it's like fate is playing a sick joke. Food and water all around and we can't access it.' I turn to Anguson to see him drinking milk from a split in his coconut. 'How did you... Never mind.' I bash the coconut again and again, and at last the damn thing splits. Milk dribbles from the crack so I hold the hairy shell to my lips and it barely satiates my thirst, but anything is better than nothing. Anguson cracks open the third coconut, again drinking the contents.

'Greedy fucker,' I grunt.

'There's plenty more.' Anguson takes another sip as I break my coconut in half.

'Aye, providing *you* can survive the next coconut gathering.'

Anguson and I dig our fingers into half-coconuts, scraping out and inhaling the white flesh. We spend the next hour or so shaking palm trees, a little more carefully, and we collect about thirty coconuts which Anguson forms into a smiley face on the beach.

Once we have eaten and drank and clogged our teeth with pulp, we collect limpets from rock pools and return to our lifeboat which is a bloody long walk away. We pluck limpets from their shells and eat these salty little snots until our stomachs are churning, and we stop before we vomit. 'Taste like crap, but *anything* makes a nice change from human flesh.' I lie flat, ready to sleep on the sand as the sun sets over the ocean.

The crashing of waves is calming until the peak of the tide tickles my feet, prompting us to move back slightly. A silhouette soars overhead and swoops seawards with bat-like wings spanning the length of five men. I sit upright as its gaping beak skims the water and then a huge splash obscures its body. Wings thrash as monstrous jaws drag the unfortunate mutant below the surface.

'You see that shit? Something just devoured an Azhdar lizard,' I say.

Anguson puffs his cheeks; sweat beading on his forehead. 'What the hell do you think it was?'

'There are only three predators I can think of that size – the sperm whale, the megalodon, and the elasmosaur. From the glimpse I caught, I'm guessing elasmosaur,' I say.

'Fuck, aren't elasmosaurs amphibious?' Anguson says.

'As far as I know, they only come ashore to lay their eggs,' I say, hoping now is not egg-laying season as I scan the waves for long necks and big teeth.

'Just as well, we wouldn't make for a light snack.' Anguson laughs monotonously. 'Still, we shouldn't stick around too long, just to be safe.'

'Yeah, we dunno what threats are out *there*,' I point to the ocean, 'and I don't fancy being fish food.'

'One upon a time the land was safer than the sea, and then the fucking mutants came. Best keep our eyes peeled,' Anguson says.

'Yup, if the last nuclear war accomplished anything, other than fifty years of peace, it made the wildlife more *interesting*. Azhdar lizards were tiny before they mutated,' I say.

'So maybe the Great War won't result in our extinction, just bring us peace, and giant koalas or hedgehogs or something?' Anguson laughs.

'Oh, it'll get a lot weirder than giant koalas with the advent of genetic engineering. I heard that scientists have created sasquatches to hunt for sport. What the fuck is wrong with these people?' I say.

'Our species aren't great at playing the Goddess,' Anguson says.

'But, of course, we're carrying out the will of the Goddess, San Teria told me so. Apparently, they were given permission by a bronze age book, fucking fools,' I say.

Anguson smiles and stares at sand grains spilling through his fingers. 'Ya reckon we're, *they're,* really winning the war like they say? It didn't take long for the Cheriton to be blown to pieces. Seems every battle results in Anatolia being on the losing side.'

'And somehow us two idiots are still alive.' I laugh, staring at the emerging stars as I think of our fallen comrades, of the dead cabin boy.

'I told you, we're not idiots, we're warriors.' Anguson flexes his shrunken bicep. 'Like it or not, men like us are built for this shit. It's the dead who aren't.'

'Well, if you ask me, we're just lucky,' I say.

Burial

For days, we splash in the soothing ocean, lounge in the tropical sun, shit in the palm forest, gorge on coconuts, shellfish, the cabin boy, appreciating the sanctuary we know cannot last. Bilton has been reduced to meat scraps on bones which smell so putrid we can no longer bare to eat the lad, but the flies are enjoying the feast.

'We should do the right thing, give him a burial. We owe him that,' I suggest, sitting before the orange orb, among scattered shells.

'Yeah, there's nothing left of him now. Best get to it. I can't look at that corpse a second longer.'

'I'll remove his shirt first. The material could come in useful.' I unzip the door flaps, kneel at the corpse in the lifeboat, undo the buttons of a military-standard shirt, and slot a shrivelled hand through a short sleeve, exposing gaping skin and vertebrae. I turn the corpse face-down and repeat the process, then rinse the shirt in the sea, failing to remove the blood stains.

Anguson and I dig through the increasingly wet sand with our bare hands until we reach buried pebbles. We carry the corpse by its fleshless limbs and lower it into the grave, taking a final look at a wrinkled grey face and smiling throat.

We cover the remains of Bilton with sand and sit in reflection with our hands on our chins. Our meat supply was once a person who did not deserve to rot in a foreign land. What a shitty situation. Poor lad never got to look upon his sister one last time, but at least she will never know he was murdered, butchered, eaten. When we return to Anatolia, I will track Mary down, tell her Bilton died a heroic death. In a way he did, saved our wretched lives anyways.

'We've stayed in mutant territory long enough. It's time we explored this place for signs of civilisation,' I suggest.

'Agreed, but fuck knows what we'll do when we find it.'

Anguson and I gather coconuts and shellfish, wrapping them in Bilton's blood-stained shirt and tying the ends, then tying the sleeves together as a strap which I hang over my shoulder.

With hand over brow, I stare at the sparkling ocean, sighing at the thought of leaving our putrid paradise. Our decision is made easier as a reptilian head rises from the waves, suspended by a long neck. It rotates like a periscope to obtain a panoramic view.

'And to answer our earlier question…' I say as the elasmosaur fixes our gaze from one hundred yards away, opening jaws which recently devoured an Azhdar lizard.

'Best hurry before it comes ashore. Good thing they're clumsy on land,' Anguson says.

The elasmosaur swims in our direction so we jog around the lifeboat and into the palm forest which provides relief from the midday sun. For hours, we travel in a straight line, swatting mosquitoes with no sense of progress among the shadowy and dazzling scenery. Birds sing a sweet song which soon grates and I could swear they are mocking our predicament.

At last, we come to a dirt road with no vehicles or hints of civilisation – there is not so much as a signpost. We turn right, not knowing whether a town lies just to our left, thanks to the endless palm trees, but at least we are not stranded on some uninhabited island.

A heatwave shimmers as I hear the hum of an engine and turn to see a motorcar from the nineteen-seventies with a big bonnet and grill. The paintwork is patchy yellow with two black stripes down the middle and I am amazed the old banger still runs.

'Should we ask for a ride?' Anguson says as we approach the roadside.

'We can't speak the language and we'd best not draw attention to the enemies in their land,' I say.

'Then what the fuck are we gonna do when we finally reach town? At some point, we're gonna have to speak to someone,' Anguson says.

The passing motorcar slows and stops just ahead with dirty smoke billowing from its exhaust. A trailer is carrying chickens in cages and I lick my lips – I could eat one of those bastards alive right now. A fat face with orange skin and black stubble pokes from the driver's window, yelling gibberish. The man is alone inside the vehicle.

Anguson and I shrug and shake our heads, standing in foreign uniforms which must be a dead giveaway to observant eyes. The driver yells more gibberish and I have no clue whether he is insulting enemies or offering a ride. Maybe he pities my bare feet because not many have shoes on the Lamantian continent.

'No, no,' Anguson says, surely clueless as to what he is declining.

'Ah, Anatolian, I knew you were outsiders. Get in. I give ride.'

Anguson and I squint at one another's sweaty, bearded faces, both thinking the same thing: Why the fuck is a Lamantian offering Anatolians a ride?

'What if he alerts the authorities?' I whisper.

'When we reach town, anyone could alert the authorities. It's a chance we have to take,' Anguson says.

'Or we could just throw him out and steal the vehicle,' I suggest, not really wanting to do that, but not prepared to rule out such action.

'And then he'd definitely *not* alert the authorities...' Anguson subtly shakes his head and we approach the striped yellow motorcar. I stare into the open window for any sudden movement, any glimpse of a weapon, but the driver's forearm remains rested on the door frame. Maybe he has Anatolian sympathies, but I cannot fathom why that would be the case. We are ruthless bastards.

'You two lost?' the man asks.

'We sure are, and a long way from home.' Anguson nods with his hands behind his back. 'We need to get home, but as you can see, we're in a dire situation. If you could take us to the nearest town, that'd be great.'

'You were walking to town? That's funny.' The man laughs robotically. 'You need place to stay? Can work farm? I pay.'

'Er, yeah, sure,' Anguson says. 'We'll need money for plane tickets. And shoes for my friend.'

'Get in back. Long ride ahead. I take farm. Hal always need workers.'

Anguson and I climb aboard the trailer, sitting between chicken cages to enjoy the stink of bird shit and exhaust fumes. Limpets rattle in Bilton's shirt as we chug through the forest on a journey to Fuck-Knows-Where.

THE RICE FARM

ANGUSON AND I BASH INTO WIRE-MESH as the dirt road gets hillier and palm trees give way to long, luscious grass swaying in the breeze. In the distance stand huge columns of tree-covered rocks which defy physics and geology. Too slender to be mountains, the furthest are obscured by atmospheric haze on an alien landscape with no sign of civilisation. Where the hell are we?

The journey is taking as long as promised, way longer than hoped for, and the clucking refuses to relent. Anguson and I are coughing from the exhaust fumes, yet the chickens have not succumbed to carbon monoxide poisoning. At last, I see the outline of buildings in the shimmering heatwave, and I hope to the Goddess this is our destination.

The nineteen-seventies motorcar stops near a large house of wood and straw, among barns and shacks which look like they would struggle to withstand a monsoon. The farmyard is all dirt, straw, and barrels with not so much as a tractor in sight. Just off-road, cows and goats inhabit a fenced area of patchy grass with many troughs, but little roaming space, and there is not a single vegetable patch. Some farm.

Anguson and I jump from the trailer onto the hot dirt, stretching our arms and shaking our legs. I undo a couple of shirt buttons and shake my collar to generate a breeze against my sweaty chest.

The man parks in a wooden shelter beside another motorcar, exits the yellow, striped vehicle, and briefly inspects the chicken cages. He is taller than the Lamantian stereotype I had envisioned, just an inch short of the towering Anguson, and he looks almost as strong, despite his advancing years.

'Is this *it?*' I scratch my head as the man leaves the shelter. 'Where's the rest?'

'Right *here.*' The man walks past the house of wood and straw, and his baggy blue shirt ripples in the breeze as he points downwards. We join him and look into a valley composed of curving silver steps which bear dozens of tiny figures, stooping and crouching. Hills spread for miles and every slope has been reconfigured in the same manner – curving silver steps apparently designed by and for giants. The process must have taken generations of labour.

'What the fuck is this?' Anguson asks as an updraft strikes my face.

'Rice fields,' the man says.

'Rice? Where the fuck's the rice?' Anguson says.

'Growing in the water.' The man points to the uppermost silver step.

'Oh, *that's* water?' Anguson says.

'Come.' The man leads us into the house of wood and straw where my soles are soothed by cool, compact dirt. His front room is dark and basic with no sign of electricity, but every wall bears cluttered shelves with more junk than anyone could keep track of. We are greeted by a lady with a rotten-toothed smile and eyes that suggest a desire to stab a knife in our throats. She is wearing a ragged, floor-length dress with flowery embroidery.

'This is my wife,' the man says in a shrill tone, sounding far-from-proud of his announcement.

'Nice to meet you,' I say and the nameless wife nods, still bearing that sexy, rotten-toothed smile.

'Wife will make food. Please take seat.'

The man gestures with his palms and we sit at a near-black table which has not been sanded, let alone varnished. My seat wobbles due to the uneven legs and then the table wobbles as I grasp the edge. A vague aroma of moss fills my nostrils as I rest our sack of limpets on the dirt floor.

The nameless wife leaves through a door composed of fibres with a wooden frame. Sunlight comes through a window hole, highlighting a tin of paint on a shelf, but I cannot see one painted wall or item of furniture. Maybe someone had good intentions but never got around to decorating.

'Me Hal. You?' The man sits at the top of the table.

'I'm er, Leo. This is… Leslie,' I say and Anguson glares across the table as I smirk. 'So, Hal, do you often pick up strangers and bring them home?'

'Only if they agree to work – we have business to run. Our staff mostly old now, need replacements.' Hal waves his finger at Anguson. 'Leslie, you look familiar. Anyone told you, you look like fighter, er… Sinney Ang-us-on.'

'I get that all the time.' Anguson scratches his bushy beard. 'I've even been asked to sign autographs!'

Hal laughs at what he assumes was a joke, and we laugh at him assuming it was a joke. The nameless wife returns and puts large plates on the table, two by two, providing a buffet of what looks like inedible crap. She places an empty wooden bowl, cup, and spoon before each seat, fills the cups with water from a jug, and sits down.

I pick a weird-shaped, battered thing from a plate and rotate it before my eyes, putting it in my mouth. It is tough, chewy, and tasteless, but I am so fucking hungry I devour one after another, washing them down with water.

'What are these things?' I ask.

'Chicken feet,' Hal says.

'Disgusting.' I munch another battered chicken foot.

Anguson and I shovel 'food' into our bowls; rice being the only thing recognisable, and we feast like we have not eaten a good meal in months.

Anyone would think we were lost at sea or something. I can feel energy replenishing my muscles and yet I cannot hold my eyelids more than half-open.

'You soldiers – I see from uniforms. Lucky we not join war yet. Still friends, sort of. You make good workers, look strong. How you get here?'

'Washed up in a lifeboat.' I yawn as the words come out.

'Oh, must've been tough time.' Hal's small, diamond eyes widen.

'Yeah, been living off shellfish and coconuts for a while now,' I say.

'You rest today, regain strength, and work tomorrow. Free food and board. Stay as long as need. Get fifty remins a week.'

'Remins? What the fuck are remins?' Anguson asks.

'Their currency, genius,' I say. 'We must've landed in Nusantara, about eight hundred miles from the Lamantian mainland.'

'Is fifty remins a lot?' Anguson picks his chipped teeth.

'Doubt it, but it's more than we have now, and we're gonna need money to get out of this place,' I say.

'And Hal's offering free chicken feet. Can't say no to that.' Anguson chuckles.

'You look tired. I take you to room. You rest now. Tomorrow, work at sunrise.'

Once our plates are empty, Hal leads us from his house into a flimsy shack which contains about twenty bunks with tweed blankets. The beds do not have mattresses or pillows and are basically wooden planks held by crooked stilts. Many have bags and ragged clothing strewn over them, and there are no ladders to the upper bunks. The air smells of stale sweat and dirt, and the only light comes from small, square window holes.

'These bunks *here* are empty so take pick.' Hal points to four bunks. 'Toilet in small hut outside. Warning, very stinky. I come wake in morning. Must go now, check on chickens.' Hal wanders from the shack and Anguson and I take the lower bunks because the upper ones would struggle to support our bulk.

Hard Labour

'TIME TO GET UP!' a voice shrieks and I open my eyes to see a small, old woman in a transparent raincoat and straw hat, standing in the light of the doorway. People are throwing off tweed blankets, rising from their beds, putting on hats and coats, and leaving the shack; their movements quick but uncoordinated as though their limbs have not woken. Anguson and I rise from our cold, hard pits no more comfortable than solid ground.

'I thought Hal was gonna wake us,' Anguson murmurs, scratching his bed-hair.

'I show you today. Hurry up,' the old woman snaps, leading us into a crowded shack which contains a bunch of spherical pots attached to string. 'Tie round waist like *this*. Make tight so not fall.' She points to the pot tied around her waist and we follow the instruction.

Men and women are taking turns pouring liquid into their pots from a white cuboid bottle with a handle. The old woman fills her pot and then ours at a long table, and she screws the lid on the bottle: 'This growth hormone. Do not spill. Expensive.'

Leaving the shack, we are led down a path between hundreds of waterlogged terraces on the hillside rice farm. As my gaze shifts left and right, we pass a woman repairing a mound of mud on a ledge to stop a leak. A few terraces lower, workers are planting green shoots directly into the water which changed from silver to brown upon approach.

'I'm exhausted already,' I mutter to no response, wiping my brow and leaning back to maintain my balance as we descend.

Halfway down the hillside, we arrive at a terrace which is not waterlogged and only a few yards wide. Green shoots, seven or eight inches tall, are poking from the mud, and slender straps of wood arch over them, serving no obvious purpose. Workers in transparent raincoats and straw hats are plucking the green shoots and tying them into bundles.

'You need to pick rice shoots, tie in bundle and place in basket. When basket filled, we carry up to terrace, apply growth hormone, and plant. It hard work.'

The old woman collects a basket from a pile stacked against the wall of the above terrace. 'Take basket and get work,' the old woman instructs, hurriedly gathering a bunch of green shoots. She removes a long stem of dry grass from her basket and ties up her bunch. 'You do same, hurry.' Anguson and I exchange glances, shrug, and pick the rice, careful not to spill our growth hormone.

Once we have filled a basket with seedlings, we head up the hillside which suddenly seems more like a mountain-face. Mosquitoes swarm around our sweaty faces and the baskets in our hands prevent us from swatting them away.

Mud squelches between my toes as we splash along a terrace half-covered with rice. The old woman places her basket on a dry mound on the inner-side, removing a bunch of green shoots. She steps into the water, dips her hand in growth hormone, wipes it on the green shoots, and plants each one into mud below the ankle-deep water.

'Come on, you do same,' she snaps, and Anguson and I obey the instruction, planting one seedling after another; neither of us anatomically suited for repeated bending.

Our shift continues in this repetitive, back-breaking manner, and we make dozens of trips up and down the hillside. Rain pours for maybe half an hour, and we discover why the others have plastic coats as our uniforms get soaked. The prospect of chicken feet and rice at least offers respite, but our ascent is precarious now the slope is wet.

We are not given the privilege of lunch in the house of wood and straw, instead led into a shack-come-canteen with the other workers. The room is sparsely-equipped with crude furniture, cupboards, and loose shelves. Window holes provide the only light, which is just as well because the unlit candles would pose a fire risk.

Hal's nameless wife serves the food alone, scooping from large bowls on a table and filling smaller bowls held by the diners. When it comes to my turn, I say: 'Just give me your finest cuisine, lovely lady,' and she serves inedible crap with a rotten-toothed smile.

Dripping wet, we sit at one of two long tables where our co-workers are eating in silence. Anguson chews loudly, talking with a full mouth: 'Any Anatolians in here?' He gets no response. 'Does anyone speak Anatolian?' A few workers glance up but say nothing. 'Talkative bunch, aren't you? Can't say I blame you. Working the hillside every day must be draining. How the fuck do you keep it up?'

'Because they're more disciplined than us lazy bastards.' I grab two wooden cups from a side-table and fill them with water from a jug, giving one to Anguson and sitting on my chair. 'I swear, a life of crime would be easier and this is only day one. Nice views, though.'

'Stop complaining,' our tiny female supervisor snaps from the next table. Anguson and I hold our spoons before our mouths and smirk at one another.

'Gotta admire the old lady's balls,' Anguson whispers. 'Not afraid to put two brutes in their place.'

'Well, I certainly wouldn't cross her.' I swallow a spoonful of rice and gulp the entire cup of water. 'Ya reckon we should stay a while to earn more money or move onto the city once we're paid?'

'First, we need to find out where the city is, or we aren't going anywhere.' Anguson raises his head. 'Hey, supervisor lady, I didn't catch your name?'

'What you want?' The old woman stops eating her rice and glares across the room.

'How far is the closest city?' Anguson says and the workers stare mid-chew; their eyes bulging in the shadows.

'City long, long way. Never been,' the old woman says.

'Is there is a bus?' Anguson says.

'No bus.'

Anguson and I exchange shrugs, then I scrape rice from my bowl and talk with a full mouth: 'I guess we'll be staying here until we can work out our next move, save as much money as we can.'

'Something tells me these wages won't get us far,' Anguson says.

'Well, anything's better than nothing and at least we have no outgoings,' I say.

'So we'll be able to save up some pocket change. If only I could access my bank account…'

When we have finished our flavoursome meal, I am tempted to call it a day, but I grudgingly return to the shift, desperate to rest. Twenty hill climbs and a growth hormone spillage later, the sun sets and our supervisor calls time. Even the spectacular view has not made the effort worthwhile.

We climb the hill and return our pots, then eat another crappy meal in the shack-come-canteen. Anguson and I stare around the candle-lit walls as our plates are collected by Hal's nameless wife. Our co-workers sit quietly or whisper like they are in a fucking library. Each gaunt, brown face somehow appears grey – their eyes empty and cheeks sagging. Poverty has taken visible effect and I cannot fathom why anyone would remain on the rice farm long term.

'What do you people do for entertainment?' Anguson asks to no reply and we stare at each other incredulously.

'What we gonna do? Spend the night twiddling our thumbs?' I say and the lack of activity in the canteen provides my answer.

'Actually, we may as well go to the sleeping quarters and finish our limpets before they go bad. I'm still starving,' Anguson says.

'Well, limpets aren't too appealing right now, but I guess we can't live off rice and chicken feet.'

Mud dries on my feet as we head to our bunks and unwrap the shirt which has filled the shack with a fishy smell. Maybe this is why no-one will talk to us. We sit on my bunk, pick limpets from their shells and place the empties into a pile on the dirt floor. Once the last limpet is gone, we look at the coconuts but lack the energy to crack them open, and Anguson lies on his bunk.

'I seriously miss my fucking penthouse, right now. And what I would do for a woman. Any woman...' Anguson says.

'I hear you. I even miss my old apartment and shitty job in McDowell's burger bar. Fuck, I might start getting sentimental,' I say.

'After lunch today it was like something awoke inside of me. Starvation must have killed any, er, desires, and then bam, I was a walking hard-on. Even the supervisor lady started to look attractive. Once we reach town, I'm seeking the nearest whorehouse, or even just a strip bar. I need something, anything, to feel human again,' Anguson says.

'Well, you've always been a walking hard-on. Months away from friends and family, and *that's* what you're concerned about,' I say.

'It's been more than months since I had a woman and *that's* hard to handle, but the real killer is sentimentality. The only option is suppression. Well, unless ya want me to start crying about the unborn child I lost, or the sister who won't speak to me,' Anguson says.

'Yeah, I miss my sister, too. Tamara is still mad about that boyfriend I chased away.' I laugh momentarily then become tense. 'We're pretty fucked up, you and me, aren't we? Two so-called tough guys, all emotionally scarred and shit.'

'Yeah, once upon a time I could unleash my frustration in the octagon. Now I don't know what I'm gonna do to stay balanced...'

Resignation

WEEKS OF LABOUR PASS. No showers. No entertainment. We collect our pay packets on Saturdays, rest on Sundays, reminisce about the authoritarian shit-hole we call home, and hope our money is not stolen while we work.

Anguson and I have earned a combined six hundred remins and have no idea whether that is enough to get us home, or even buy a pair of shoes. My feet constantly itch and the skin is flaking from prolonged exposure to moisture in the rice terraces. I swear they are infected with some nasty shit, and in a land like Nusantara, medical treatment is likely a non-starter. If I stay much longer, I fear my feet may rot and fall off.

At midday, Anguson and I struggle up the hillside in rain to 'enjoy' our meal of chicken feet and rice. And as we sit in the canteen, my lower back is so stiff I do not think I can return to my shift. The old women labouring on the rice terraces make me feel so inadequate.

'What I don't understand is why we pick shoots just to plant them again elsewhere. What's the point in that?' I whisper as we eat lunch; my hand trembling from lack of energy.

'No fucking idea. I just know we're getting paid for it so I don't ask questions,' Anguson says. 'I dunno how these skinny fuckers do it, though. To think, this hillside is their entire lives. I must admit I'm struggling now, and the way we're chastised for shirking…'

'Well, we had more than enough orders in the military and my back is getting stiffer by the day. At this rate, I'm gonna be an invalid.' I sigh.

'I reckon we find Hal, collect our final pay packet, and get the fuck out of here. Head for the nearest city. Surely, we've earned enough to get home,' Anguson says.

'Music to my ears, I tell ya. Let's do it.' I sit upright with a sudden burst of energy. 'First thing we do when we reach the city – find a pub. I'm dying for a pint.'

'And then a titty bar.' Anguson grins widely. 'Don't forget the titty bar.'

Anguson and I leave the canteen, collect our money from under our tweed blankets, and approach the house of wood and straw. Yelling is coming from inside the building so I glance to Anguson. 'Sounds like a domestic.' We wait at the door, crossing our arms, tapping our feet, staring at the shacks and the paddock, sighing, and still the yelling continues. The only voice is that of Hal's. 'Old bastard has a temper on him.'

I push open the door of woven fibres, enter the dark lobby, and peer through an ajar door. Beyond the dining table, an old-ish female worker is cowering in her raincoat, trembling. She drops to one knee as Hal whips her shoulder with a strap of wood. Anguson marches into the room and I suspect Hal is going to discover 'Leslie' is not a lookalike of the infamous cage-fighter.

Hal steps back from his victim, gawping to reveal missing teeth as his face reddens. 'What you doing in here, Leslie? This not concern you. Woman break–'

Anguson snatches the wooden strap and strikes Hal with one of his legendary haymakers. The old bastard crashes onto his dining table, smashing it to pieces and landing flat on his back. Anguson tosses the strap and places his hands on his hips. The woman is still crouching as though she needs permission to stand.

'There is *no* excuse for hitting a woman, you damn coward. I was planning on leaving on friendly terms, but you've just made me change my mind. I want the keys to a vehicle, money, food, and water. Now!'

Hal lies among broken wood with a split lip and bloodied whiskers, shuffling backwards. He turns onto his knees and stands on wobbly legs inside a dust cloud. Shaking, he rummages through a grey dresser, removes a pile of money, and hands the notes to Anguson.

'Wife! Wife!' Hal yells and his nameless wife shuffles into the front room in her ragged dress. We are not greeted by a rotten-toothed smile this time. 'I need you to pack food and water in car for these good men. Here keys.' Hal tosses the keys to his wife, which she catches in two hands, and she shuffles from the room. Her lack of alarm suggests she is all-too-familiar with her husband's aggressive behaviour.

'You wanna come with us? We can take you home,' I say to the abused female worker as she slowly rises.

'This her home. She no speak Anatolian. Nowhere to go,' Hal says.

'In that case, order her to slap you.' I smirk, staring at Hal with short nods.

'Wh-what?'

'You heard me.' I cross my arms and raise my chin. Hal mutters in his native tongue and the woman's eyes bulge from behind her flopping black hair. She glances to her rescuers and then to Hal with her arms pressed against her frail body.

'Tell her to hit you, or Sydney Anguson will hit you again. And next time he won't pull his punch,' I say.

'You real Sinney Ang-us-on? I knew it,' Hal gasps.

I point to the woman who is now a statue, and my eyes shift between the pair, then I nod at her. Hal mutters in his native tongue; his fat face sweating, small eyes shrinking into a squint. The woman raises her hand and gently slaps Hal who turns his cheek; his broad chest heaving in his baggy blue shirt.

'Again, harder,' I say and Hal relays the instruction in a whisper, prompting the woman to slap with increasing and amusing force. *Slap. Slap. Slap.* Anguson and I erupt into laughter as Hal cowers, whimpering. 'That'll do. I take it you've learnt your lesson, you bullying bastard?'

'Y-yes.' Hal holds his cheek, pouting.

'Okay, lead us to the vehicle and do not think of bullying your workers again. Never know when karma will bite you,' I say.

Anguson places a few remin notes into the woman's trembling hand and Hal leads us into his large wooden shelter with no front wall. It contains one trailer, two rusty cars and two rustier motorbikes; each more than half a century old. The nameless wife places the last hamper into the boot, slams it shut, and Anguson snatches the keys from her grasp.

'Where's the nearest town?' I ask.

'Batavia is hundred miles in *that* direction, beyond hills,' Hal says.

'The capital… So we may at last catch sight of civilisation,' I say.

THE 'HOTEL'

USING A GEAR STICK for the first time in years, I drive the old banger through the Nusantaran hills, admiring endless silver terraces. A smile is fixed to my face, but my relief is tinged by the concern Hal's victim may become a target, thanks to our intervention. I doubt the poor woman is grateful for the few remins her boss will likely reclaim.

The undulation of the road makes the one hundred miles to the capital seem a hell of a lot longer, but from the final peak we see a glorious sight on the horizon – an unmistakable silhouette of one of planet Eryx's most populous cities.

'Civilisation, at last.' I sigh.

'Can't believe I'm excited to see an industrialised shithole. Place is almost as ugly as Mydilsburgh,' Anguson says.

'This *shithole* looks like fucking paradise from where I'm sitting,' I say.

'My idea of paradise is anywhere that serves beer. And the pleasant scenery will be a nice reminder of our training days. Put your foot down, Leo,' Anguson says with a hint of sarcasm and I weave through the light traffic at high speed.

We reach Batavia, driving through an area with buildings ten or more storeys tall, but not much more than shacks in terms of build quality. Some are constructed from bricks and mortar, others from wood, all just waiting to be razed by an earthquake. Filthy banners are hanging from horizontal poles and hundreds of power cables crisscross overhead. Wooden balconies are hanging, or rather dangling, from the faces of buildings, somehow staying up, and I would not fancy admiring the view from up there.

We pass beige flats with wooden shutters, scanning for anything resembling a hotel as shops and restaurants come into view. A concrete building has a lobby visible through the glass doorway – and this establishment seems to be a higher class than most in the area. The electronic red and yellow sign above the entrance looks hotel-ish, and a person is leaving with a suitcase so I drive into a car park at the rear.

'You'll need to get out, book us a room. I can't just walk up to reception in bare feet. They'll assume I'm a peasant and call the cops,' I say.

'But if I walk in there, I might be recognised, especially if they hear me speaking Anatolian,' Anguson says.

'Your hair and beard are so long I barely recognise you, and your tan makes you appear Lamantian. You're almost as brown as me, now. Just walk in there, put some money on the counter and mutter gibberish. They won't know what language you're speaking. They'll just hand over a sign-in form and give you the room key. Once you've checked in, I'll sneak in behind you and hope no-one spots my rotting feet.'

I sit in the vehicle, staring at the dials on the wooden dashboard as Anguson heads into the hotel. A minute or so later, I get out, lock the door, and head onto the busy street where a few pedestrians are also barefoot. I peer through the glass doorway where Anguson is gesticulating theatrically and I have no idea what the oaf is saying. A receptionist slides a form and pen across the desk, and Anguson signs his name, then snatches a key-card. I enter the hotel, sneaking across the lobby to the stairway which contains a golden placard with many symbols.

'Which floor?' I ask.

'No fucking clue, but this card has a symbol on it. Let's look for the door with the matching symbol.'

Anguson and I pass through a pine door into a corridor which reveals an unexpected type of accommodation. The corridor is lined with two rows of square glass doors on either side, one on top of another. Long steel handles are fixed between the top and bottom doors, and beyond the glass are beds. Just beds. The rooms are basically capsules containing beds.

'There is no way I am sharing one of these with you,' I mutter.

'These damn things are expensive and we have to save money. Quit your complaining,' Anguson snaps and we follow the corridor, checking for a capsule with a symbol matching the key-card without success. We ascend the stairs to the next floor where we locate our symbol on one of the higher windows.

'How the fuck do I reach?' Anguson stands on tiptoes, not quite reaching the card slot which would be way out of reach of the average person.

'What about this?' I point to a metal handle below the door which Anguson gently pulls as he steps back. A wide step-ladder extends outwards and then automatically reaches the plush blue carpet. Anguson climbs the steps, swipes the key-card, and the flexible door is sucked into a slit, beeping. Anguson climbs into a capsule designed for much smaller people and says: 'Come and check this out. It has a compuscreen.'

As I enter the capsule, I say: 'Okay, how do I close this thing?' and then I notice a silver, square button beside the doorway. I press the button and the flexiglass door emerges from its slot, beeping as it slowly closes. At the same time, the retractable step-ladder folds away and returns to its slot. I pull a curtain to give us privacy and crawl towards the back wall which displays a glowing picture of planet Eryx. The other walls are grey and featureless apart from small shelves and a plug socket. I sit at the top of the bed, facing a compuscreen hanging from the ceiling.

'Who should we contact?' Anguson asks.

'Type an email and send it to everyone in your address book if need be. We need someone to tell us how we can get off this damn island and cross twelve thousand miles of ocean.'

Anguson activates the compuscreen – a curving touchscreen device with an up-facing virtual keyboard and a two-dimensional display. He toggles to the Anatolian language settings, logs into his email account and types:

I'm in Nusantara, currently in the capital Batavia. Our ship was sunk. Only me and Leo Jardine made it into our lifeboat. I don't know how many others survived. We're stranded and need help. I'm guessing there aren't too many flights between Nusantara and Anatolia, given that we're at war with their neighbours. If anyone has suggestions, or can go one better and send rescue that would be helpful.

Sydney

Anguson sends the email to every contact in his address book and logs out of his account, opening a new window in the browser. It defaults to a news page showing an image of Nyberu's prime bombing target – Skye City – a recently constructed tri-tower reaching two miles above Anatolia's capital Medio.

'While we wait for replies, you'd better get me a pair of shoes. In fact, get us some new clothes, given that we're in military uniform. While you're gone, I'll send an email of my own.'

'What shoe size?' Anguson says.

'Fourteen,' I say.

'Same size as me… Clothes?'

'About the same as you.'

'Really? You're fatter than me.'

'And a couple of inches shorter, genius.'

Anguson opens the curtain, hits the silver, square button, and climbs down the retractable step-ladder. I close the door and curtain, email everyone in my address book, and rest on a pillow embroidered with plant stems as I drift away. This is way cosier than our cabin on the STS Cheriton…

Sometime later, I am awoken by beeping and Anguson climbs into the capsule with a couple of shopping bags and a wicker basket. He presses the silver, square button to close the glass door, and says: 'Two new outfits, clean underwear, and a pair of shoes. Had to walk for bloody ages to get these.'

Anguson digs into a hamper prepared by Hal's nameless wife, munching chicken feet which are hopefully not laced with poison. *'That* one's yours.' Anguson points to a large, stuffed bag which I collect as I crawl to the door.

'Now to find the showers. I must get rid of this smell for the sake of the other guests,' I say.

'I think there are showers at the end of the corridor,' Anguson says.

'You didn't buy towels by any chance?' I say.

'No, we need to save money. Just shake yourself dry like the dog you are,' Anguson says.

I climb from the capsule with my carrier bag, pass a guest on a step ladder, and reach the end of the corridor. Standing in a small lobby, I shrug and take a guess, opening a door to see a woman glaring from a changing room, thankfully fully clothed. Seriously, why do the placards not contain universal gender symbols?

Spinning around, I proceed into the opposite door before the police are called. Urinals confirm this is the men's room so I pass the unused coat-hooks and enter a shower cubicle. Placing my bag down, I strip my military uniform and wash months of grease from my skin in scorching hot water. Such relief.

Human again, I climb out of the shower, put on clean white socks and underpants, then hold up my new clothes and curl my lips. Someone thinks he is a comedian. I get dressed in a pink shirt with palm trees and pineapples, and then a pair of green shorts with daisies. Fucking daisies. I am not relishing opening my shoe box.

Nevertheless, I lift the lid and remove tissue-paper to see sandals not dissimilar to those worn by the prophet Samaris. I put the sandals on over my white socks, put the dirty uniform into the shopping bag, and return to the capsule, ready to commit murder.

Anguson is smugly awaiting my return, sitting with his legs dangling from the capsule doorway. The cage-fighter points and howls with laughter as I glare, standing stiffly in these ridiculous clothes. It takes him a good sixty seconds to compose himself, and then he says: 'Okay, I'm done checking my emails. Time to take a shower.'

I climb into the capsule and check my email notifications, hoping to receive a reply from one person more than any other – my younger sister Tamara. Three times, I scroll through the spam folder and the replies from others, but there is nothing. I guess she still hates me, and who can blame her? I was such an overbearing bastard after our father was murdered, but that was my way of protecting her.

I read through my email replies and the most useful is from an old friend who escaped the Medio slums and obtained Level Two Citizenship – a rare achievement.

Well, it's good to hear you're alive, Leo. I'm sorry to say our friend Seth is no longer with us. Killed on the front line. He was a good lad.

The best I can suggest is to travel to Scania, one of the few neutral territories in this war. From there you should be able to take a flight to Anatolia. You'll need to get out of Nusantara fast. Rumour has it they're going to join the war any day. Their allegiance lies with Nyberu and they've always distrusted Anatolians. Do not reveal your identity or you two could be imprisoned. Or worse. A celebrity POW like Sydney Anguson would be great PR.

Jackson

Remins are sitting on the shelf so I add mine to the pile and attempt to count the notes. I have a vague idea of their value from my familiarity with our pay packets, but Hal could have been ripping us off for all we know. Every week, he gave us two notes bearing an eagle and one bearing a rooster, totalling fifty remins. We have thirty-six of what I believe are twenty-remin notes and twenty-four of what I believe are ten-remin notes as well as a few unfamiliar notes.

As I check the cost of flights on the compuscreen, Anguson returns to the capsule in a pin-stripe suit and black leather shoes. Sitting against the wall, he holds his damp beard, turns sideways and pouts.

'Oh, so you *do* have a sense of style… Just not when it comes to buying for me.' Anguson laughs proudly and I do not return his gaze. 'So we need to fly to Scania and then to Anatolia. I've just checked online and we're talking five thousand remins for the plane tickets.'

'Let's find the nearest Hewitt's bank,' Anguson says.

'Without ID, a debit card, or even a branch in this country, there's no chance of that,' I say.

'Fuck, this is so frustrating.' Anguson clenches his teeth.

'As far as I can tell, we've got about a thousand remins left, not that I can read the numbers on the notes. Where we gonna get another four thousand remins?'

'The only realistic plan is robbery,' Anguson says and we both lower our gaze.

'Robbery? Fuck, I thought we'd left those days behind. We're not starving slum kids anymore,' I murmur.

'No, we're desperate men in an enemy land. I say we go out tonight, look for drunk people heading home from the pub alone. Take their wallets. They'll be easy prey. Just look out for cops.'

Desperate Times...

LATE IN THE EVENING, Anguson and I explore streets swarming with peasants who are not segregated like in Anatolia. Our armpits are lacking the usual stench as we make a bold fashion statement with our bushy beards and wild hair. And of course, my dazzling floral shorts, pineapple shirt, and Samaris sandals.

Black clouds are glowing orange-brown at frayed edges from the light of two moons. The tainted wind is itching my nostrils; dust and fumes obscuring visibility like a sandstorm, smearing the traffic lights which double as navigation beacons. Shouting voices, loud, barely out of adolescence take on the tone of squawking crows. We trample over patches of chewing gum on uneven concrete with embedded stones, but soon the pavement changes to grey slabs.

The streets of the city centre are a stark contrast to the slums in the outskirts, visually, if not morally. Neon signs and holograms depict logos and product images stretching into the night sky; one classy establishment has a big, bright display of titties in the window.

Pedestrians stagger around, laugh, quarrel, glare like they could take on a champion cage-fighter. Fucking fools. Occasionally I glimpse a metal hand, a red iris on those who purchased low-grade cybernetics to act the tough guy. Real technology has not reached this part of the world and the underground 'surgeons' cannot correctly implant this shit, let alone fix it when things go wrong. Infections, mechanical failures, and coordination issues arising from bad wiring are commonplace. A man with metal horns on his temples and one arm passes by, and I am guessing bodged limb replacement. Stupid bastard hopefully learnt his lesson.

At the end of the road, a half-naked woman leans towards passers-by; titties hanging out of black lace that can barely be considered a top as she puffs a cigarette.

'That's it.' I glance to Anguson. 'Hookers always have money. Escort her into an alley, take her fucking purse, then move onto another area before her pimp gives us aggro.'

'Don't look at me.' Anguson shrugs and bears his palms. 'If you want to rob a woman, be my fucking guest.'

'I don't wan... Never mind. Just wait for me.'

Weaving through bodies, I march along the street to meet the hooker others are avoiding. She reveals her big titties as she leans towards me, smiling from a makeup-free face younger and less repugnant than expected, but not quite pretty. She mutters gibberish in a masculine voice, possibly ladyboy, and I nod, following her into an alley where the air is calmer, but the stench of piss is strong.

We pass through a flaking wooden gate into a small yard, behind a bar, which contains a couple of bins, a black iron door, and nothing else. The hooker flicks her cigarette, closes the gate, and mutters more gibberish in her masculine voice. I hold my curled fingers to my mouth and stick my tongue in my cheek. She drops to her knees, pulls down my floral shorts and gives me my first blowjob for a long fucking time. Staring at the twin moons, I shoot my load earlier than anticipated and grab the woman's handbag as she spits cum onto the concrete.

The hooker yells so I grab her neck, not too hard, and place a finger over my lips. I open her purse and pull out every note, chucking it to the ground and fleeing the alley as the hooker yells again. I reunite with Anguson on the main street and we quickly march onto another area before her pimp emerges. Not that we are afraid.

Rain pours and the forming puddles paint the road pink, blue, and purple against a shiny, rippling black. I can barely hear Anguson speaking due to the music booming out of pubs, splashing rain, excitable voices, the hissing of wheel spray... I just nod in agreement.

Groups of girls giggle arm-in-arm, and every mini-skirt and low-cut top brings a smile – fat girls, skinny ones, athletic ones, buxom ones, inviting my eyes and then glaring when the invitation is accepted.

As we approach a telephone booth bearing fluorescent adverts, Anguson and I turn off the busy street, heading through an alley of barred windows and crimson bricks. Cigarette butts float in water between cobblestones, jumping in response to our splashing feet. A lone man staggers by discarded boxes and garbage cans; his saturated orange shirt clinging to his skin.

Upon passing our youthful prey, two brutes grab a skinny forearm each without resistance. Anguson removes the man's wallet from his trouser pocket and his face wilts like his skin is melting. We release his forearms and the man splashes towards the refuge of the drunks on the main street.

'Look at us, robbing people as poor as we are, like teenage thugs,' Anguson mutters; rain dripping from his beard.

'It doesn't feel good, but what choice have we got?' I ask and Anguson hesitates, shaking his stooped head.

'Well, I've had enough shame for one night. Let's get out of the rain and grab a beer.' Anguson removes a few notes from the stolen wallet and tosses it onto the cobblestones.

'Ah beer... I haven't tasted sweet, sweet beer in far too long.'

Anguson and I enter a strip club for long-awaited relaxation, enticed by the titty-shaped lights in the window. I approach the bar, point to beer taps, raise two fingers, and hand a note to the barmaid. Collecting my change and two pints, I join Anguson at a round table in a prime viewing location. As I sit back, Anguson says: 'To our fallen comrades,' and we clink our glasses together.

Lilac lights sweep through the shadows, revealing note-filled garters and pert titties. A grin is welded to my face because I have not seen a naked lady in so long even Anguson was looking attractive, the rugged, handsome bastard! I place the pint glass to my sunburnt lips, and a sip of beer provides my second orgasm of the night, well, not literally. I notice Anguson eyeing the notes pressed against a skinny thigh and mutter: 'Don't even think about it.'

'Giving them money or taking their money?' Anguson says.

'Both.' I belch and stare at the golden liquid in my pint glass.

'Fucking titties, eh? I swear this is like therapy right now – exorcising the demons of war, celebrating the memory of good men,' Anguson says.

'Yeah, I'm sure they'll be touched by the sentiment.' I gulp beer and wipe the froth from my beard.

'We're gonna need to get out there soon. If we don't make enough to cover our hotel bill and more, we're wasting our time,' Anguson says.

'We'll need to count the money properly this time. Back at the hotel, we can look up the symbols on the CUS. See how they relate to Anatolian numbers,' I say.

'We could do with weapons, too. Maybe find an arms dealer,' Anguson says. 'Sooner or later, we could get in trouble. Rob the wrong civilian, they could pull a gun, call their friends, the police. Even I can't depend on my fists all the time.'

'It's fucked up, robbing these people. The speeches I've made about how the poor must unite… Nusantarans are just another race exploited by Anatolia for cheap labour. And now they're paying for our plane tickets,' I say.

'Funny, this land isn't as backwards as I expected. From where I'm sitting, it's pretty much the same as home. Millions of piss poor people, shiny city centres, and a handful of rich bastards like me,' Anguson says.

'The only difference is our rich are slightly richer and our poor wear the clothes made by their poor.' I take a couple of gulps, nearing the end of my pint.

'And now their poor are getting hold of our cybernetics. It's a changing world. Every fucker is gonna go transhuman soon,' Anguson says.

'Transhuman – now there's a fucking word. Replace your humanity with recycled scrapyard junk and tell yourself you're something better,' I say.

'Even people like you will succumb one day, Jardine.'

'Nah, I'll never go for that shit. And I dunno why you sound so enthused. Even the best cybernetic arm on the market isn't gonna match the Sydney Anguson right. If you ask me, cybernetics is a false dawn – biotech is the next big thing. Why replace you've got, if you can just make it better? Twenty years from now, people will swallow a pill to rewrite their DNA, make 'em as strong as you.'

'Someone's been watching too many sci-fi movies.' Anguson tenses his forearm, laughing as his muscles almost tear through the naked lady tattoo revealed by his rolled-up shirt sleeve. 'One more beer and we'll get back to street thuggery.'

Anguson and I down another pint each, and the cage-fighter smacks a stripper's arse on our way out the bar. She places her long fingernails over her mouth as her cheeks jiggle. A short and stocky bouncer, almost cube-like in stature, approaches Anguson, stares into those cold brown eyes and thinks better of it. A six feet seven inch, muscular brute would be hard work, even if he was not a trained martial artist.

On our way back to the capsule hotel, Anguson and I rob another four 'innocent' people, and I feel a part of my conscience die each time. This is necessary shit. Greater good and all that.

Shopping Trip

THE NEXT DAY, Anguson and I explore the bustling centre of Batavia, seeking an arms dealer so we can step up our robbery game. Dazzling glass towers stretch into the sky, joined by glass walkways, but at ground-level things are not so high-tech and flea markets are regular sights. We pass roadside sellers and I inhale the smell of cooked food, but lose my appetite at a stall with deep-fried rats hanging from string.

We reach a public square with a five-chain tall statue of the Jebedan God Ceros – a golden man with a rhinoceros head, wielding a long-sword and round shield. This mighty deity could slice the surrounding skyscrapers in half with one swipe of that gleaming sword.

'Just like looking in a mirror,' Anguson mutters as he stares at Ceros' bulging abdominals.

'Comparing yourself a rhinoceros?' I say.

'What, er, no, just the muscles. If I was wearing a mask or something…' Anguson mumbles and I laugh through my nose.

'I'm sure the Gods are astounded by the similarity.'

As we walk between Ceros' legs, the detailing of his boots, calf muscles, and veins is impressively accurate. No wonder they call this statue one of the Wonders of Eryx.

We leave the flawless white town square, crossing a road lined with parked cars plugged into power points. A store with a barred window catches my eye and upon approach, I see a display of guns ranging from antique to state of the art. A bell rings as we enter an armoury as well-stocked as any in Anatolia with weapons covering every wall. Behind the counter, a man with metal horns yawns to reveal fangs and a forked tongue.

We peruse the items on display; many designs are unfamiliar, but others are instantly recognisable – the KAL 10 Machine Pistol, the Elsar Pulse Phaser, the Kansdale Electro-Magnetic Rail Gun.

'Check out this beauty.' Anguson points to a sleek chrome weapon with a red stripe on the barrel. 'The Bolo-Vela GRB. Fires an energy beam as hot as the centre of the Sun. Banned from sale back home due to safety and practicality issues. Shoot this bad girl into a crowd, it'll burn a hole straight through ten people like they aren't there.'

'A little OTT for what we've got planned, don't ya think?' I say.

'I know, but a soldier can dream…' Anguson says.

'Let's just pick up a couple of KAL 10's and be on our way.' I point to the KAL 10 on the wall and raise two fingers. The seller reaches below his counter and collects two boxes with images of machine pistols on the front, placing them before us. He holds up a box of ammunition and I raise one finger, then he places the box on the counter. I point to a chest holster in a glass cabinet, raise two fingers, and the man adds them to our collection.

He mutters gibberish and I spread remin notes over the white plastic counter for him to count. I add notes one by one, looking to the seller each time, and finally he grabs my wrist and raises his palm. He puts the money in the till, then places the boxes into fabric bags which he hands over. Anguson and I leave the store, now the not-so-proud owners of machine pistols.

'These things are perfect if we find ourselves in a bind, but for fuck's sake, do not get trigger-happy. We don't want civilian blood on our hands,' I say.

'So we get new toys, but we don't get to use them?' Anguson says.

'Don't worry, tough guy, you'll still get to wave yours around and scare the ladies. Just no shooting your load, okay?'

Anguson and I return to the capsule hotel and unpackage our new toys which are compact, rectangular, and crude. I run my finger through one of two grooves on the barrel, then fix a clip into the handle, just in case. I remove my shirt and strap on my chest holster, slotting in the KAL 10 and two clips of ammunition. Suddenly, I feel like a soldier again.

Dinner Date

Anguson and I sit in our grey capsule among gun packaging, facing the ceiling-mounted compuscreen, and I toggle to the Anatolian version of the virtual keyboard. I run a search on Nusantaran numbers and sort our notes into matching piles to calculate how much money we have left, having splurged about half.

'So this symbol is twenty and we have twenty-seven of those, that's five-forty. Thirty tens are three-hundred, er, eight-forty. Three fives and some change. We have a little over eight-hundred-and-fifty-five remins. In other words, we're no further forwards.'

'And what's eight-hundred-and-fifty-five remins in real money?' Anguson says.

'Let's check.' I run an internet search on the compuscreen for the exchange rate and type *855* into the online calculator. 'Three-hundred-and-seventy-two Anatolian credits.'

'Are you kidding me? All that work for three-hundred-and-seventy-two credits. Fuck's sake,' Anguson says.

'Calm down. One good robbery could give us all the money we need to get home.' I stuff the notes into my wallet and put the gun packaging into the bag.

'So what's the next target?' Anguson says.

'Well, I've been thinking hookers–'

'Have you lost your mind? We just bought guns so we could move past robbing hookers.'

'If you let me finish,' I take a deep breath, 'I was gonna suggest driving around the streets and watching out for pimps collecting their dues. Then we jump out the vehicle and rob the motherfucker. That way we don't have to worry about guilt, and one or two robberies might be all we need.'

'That's assuming they collect their dues in the street. I dunno about you, but I have no clue how pimps operate.' Anguson pauses and shuffles on the bed. 'Anyways, I suppose it's worth a try…'

Anguson and I rest for a while, against opposite walls in the capsule, still just inches from one another, and I cannot sleep due to the cage-fighter's drill-like snoring. We get showered and changed, and my new outfit is just as garish as the previous one – butterflies and rainbows this time. Thanks Anguson.

We bin our gun packaging, take our clothes to a laundry room, slot a coin into the washing machine, and load our sweaty clothes, uniforms included.

Leaving the hotel fully-armed, we head into a restaurant with wood-panelled walls and customers eating edible-looking food. We take a corner-table with a window view, browsing the menu as pedestrians walk back and forth. The restaurant is decorated in dull yellows, greens, and browns, but looks semi-hygienic, at least. I say that because the window-sill is dust-free, but bears two dead bluebottles.

'Oh my Goddess, I don't believe it, the menu has fucking pictures. I actually know what I'm ordering here.' Anguson points to a dish on the menu. 'That's chicken, isn't it? Better be fucking chicken, and no feet either. That's what I'm ordering, chicken and rice and peas and shit.' Anguson sits back, eyes half-closed, jaw hanging open, and I could swear the thought of chicken has aroused him.

As I look up from the menu, a tin-can on wheels whizzes between the packed tables and abruptly stops. It stands before us with four snake-like arms, a big square smile, and cartoon eyes on its cylindrical body. The service droid mutters gibberish in a cheerful voice as Anguson and I exchange grins.

'They have droids in this part of the world? Nusantara is really catching up,' Anguson says.

'Crappiest droid I've ever seen,' I reply and laughter splutters from our lips.

'Sirs, please, you'll hurt my feelings.' The pitch of the droid's voice rises and we roar with laughter, attracting stares from the other diners. 'Are you ready to order?'

'I'm impressed, it talks Anatolian.' Anguson slaps the brown plastic table and the condiments wobble.

'And one hundred and seventy nine other languages. Now, if you don't mind, I'll return when you're ready to order.' The service droid spins on tiny wheels and cruises towards another table.

'Wait, we're ready now,' Anguson insists and the droid turns back, placing its hands where hips would be situated on a human. 'I'll have this chicken and shit, this one *here.*'

'If you would kindly mind your language, sir, and a *please* would be nice.'

'Oh sorry, er, please.' Anguson blushes as I laugh again, and the service droid's big round eyes close into a glare of sorts. *As if* it has metal eyelids.

'I'll have the same as him, please, waiter.' I clasp my hands and shuffle my backside.

'Any drinks?' the service droid asks.

'Beer,' Anguson and I say together, nodding.

'No problem, sirs, I'll bring the beers right over. Food shouldn't be too long.' The service droid whizzes over mustard tiles and enters a door, revealing chefs at work in the steamy kitchen.

'Giant statues, robotic waiters, this place gets more like home by the minute,' Anguson says.

'Only their robots are crappier than ours and their gods are cooler. A giant sword and rhino head, I mean, damn, I'm not a religious man, but if I was gonna get behind a god, it would be Ceros all day,' I say.

'Ceros – the God whose body bears a stark resemblance to mine – isn't he a tyrant?' Anguson squints one eye.

'Aren't they all? This guy's just honest about it. If he's gonna crush you, he doesn't dress it up with morality and shit, he just crushes you like the bug you are.'

'Sounds like he'd be a perfect match for San Teria.' Anguson bears his teeth, nodding subtly.

'Nah, not deceitful enough. San Teria are full of cowshit, just like their Goddess. They kill *out of love*.'

The service droid returns with glasses in all four hands and places our beers onto coasters. 'Your drinks, sirs,' it says and then whizzes to another table to serve pink and blue cocktails. Anguson and I raise our pint glasses, gulping beer and gasping as my tongue tingles.

'So people can have access to droids, cybernetics and gadgetry, and still go hungry.' Anguson tilts his head and scratches the top of his cheek.

'It's economics. Convince people they need your product, some will find a way to get it, even at the expense of stuff they need. We blame the Elites for poverty, but stupidity plays its role,' I say.

'Aye, the poor should refuse to play their games, but they can never resist. Fucking puppets,' Anguson says.

'Exactly. Take cybernetics for example. People are signing credit agreements to get replacement arms and feel like tough guys. For a poor person, this would be the equivalent of taking out a mortgage; they'll be making the repayments for twenty years. Once the cybernetics are implanted, they have no choice but to make the repayments, otherwise the parts are removed and they don't get their old arms back. This means they'll beg, steal, and starve in order to make the repayments.

'People who can't afford basic luxuries are turning themselves into fucking cyborgs, and they're so gullible, they don't realise the low-cost upgrades they're purchasing are only cheap because they're the lowest quality possible. I mean some are even recycled removals. Someone else didn't keep up the repayments and now their arm is your arm. It's fucking creepy.'

'When you put it like that…' Anguson stares at his knuckles. 'If I didn't have a career to return to, I'd still be tempted, though.'

'Why? All legal cybernetics are strength-limited and wouldn't make you much stronger than the average man. Sure, a metal hand is a little tougher than a flesh and bone one, but you're five times stronger than the average man. It would be a downgrade.'

'So I'd go illegal.' Anguson shrugs, pouting his bottom lip.

'Have you listened to a word I said? Illegal implants malfunction all the time, and it's not like you can just ask for a refund. Shit, some of them don't even function in bad weather. Gets a bit cold, suddenly you can't move your fingers.'

'But I could warm up and break someone's face with my iron knuckles.' Anguson raises his huge, tattooed fist.

'Well, there is that.' I laugh as a delicious smell wafts in my direction and I glance to the service droid bringing our dinner. It places our plates onto the brown plastic table, saying: 'Enjoy your meals,' and Anguson and I eat the chicken and rice and peas and shit.

THE PIMP HUNT

IN THE EARLY HOURS, we tour the sleazier side of town in our nineteen-seventies motorcar, driving by any corner worked by a hooker.

After an hour of thigh and cleavage flashes, we reach an area near a monument and train station which has plenty of foot traffic. I lower my window as a hooded man approaches a hooker, following her past drunks into a dark alley. 'It's either a punter or a pimp. Only one way to find out.' I stop at traffic lights, Anguson jumps out the vehicle, and I U-turn as my accomplice interrupts their liaison.

I park in the light of a fast-food shop, waiting nervously until Anguson runs from the alley and hurdles a roadside fence. He jumps into the passenger door, withdraws a few notes and tosses a wallet from the window. Driving off, I check the rear-view mirror for signs of police but see only two drunks crossing the road.

'Fucking punter, burst into tears the moment I emerged. Didn't even have to pull my gun.'

'Well, you should've had it ready anyways, dumb arse. What if a pimp pulled on you?' I say.

'He would've met the famous Sydney Anguson right.'

'And you're the one who suggested buying guns…'

Anguson and I spend another hour patrolling Batavia for hookers who are having a frustratingly quiet night. Losing patience with the city centre, we reach the run-down area with shack-like towers, spotting a hooker standing in an empty street. She is staring along the broken tarmac with watery eyes bearing an unexpected innocence. I am guessing she is a teenage girl unaccustomed to the harsh reality of street-walking. She will need to harden if she is to last.

'I say just park here and see what happens with her. She's getting no action so I reckon the next guy who comes along will be her pimp, assuming he comes along.' I drive between two buildings with shuttered windows, parking below the stairs of a fire escape. The hooker is just visible at the end of the road, standing with arms across her chest, breathing heavily. Given how quiet this area is, she must surely be expecting her employer to pay her a visit.

Fifteen minutes pass. A man in a leather jacket walks briskly along the path, passes the hooker and nods over his shoulder. She touches her mid-length black hair, looks both ways, then follows him around the corner.

'Okay, your turn,' Anguson says.

'But I'm the getaway driv–'

'Just go, will ya?'

Unbuttoning my top shirt buttons, I get out the motorcar and hurry down the road, passing the steps of apartment buildings. I turn the corner to see the man marching down the street with the hooker following ten yards behind. Jogging towards my targets, I withdraw the machine pistol from my chest holster and yell: 'Stop.'

The man spins around and reaches into his leather jacket, freezing as I point a finger and shake my head. He slowly raises his hands, tilting his shaven head, almost patronisingly. The hooker steps back and I twice flick my hand in the direction of her pimp. Her high-heel wobbles as she walks over to him, backwards.

I approach with a gun aimed at a face bearing a slender moustache and confident eyes which suggest the pimp is familiar with this position. The hooker shakes like her next fix is overdue.

I point to the hooker's black and gold handbag and gesture to the stony path with my free hand. She tosses the handbag as instructed. I then point to the pimp's brown leather jacket and aggressively repeat the gesture. He raises his slanted eyebrows and slowly reaches into his inner-pocket. My finger is resting on the trigger, ready to squeeze at the first glint of steel.

The pimp removes his wallet, holds it to the streetlight and tosses it next to the handbag. I twice flick my wrist and the pair scurry along the street as I collect the items.

Anguson cruises along the road so I run towards the vehicle and BANG! BANG! The rear-side window explodes as a searing pain engulfs my right forearm. I drop my acquisitions, spin around and spray fire as the pimp leaps further than any regular human could.

The hooker runs from the crossfire as I drop flat; my bullets peeling skin from the pimp's face to reveal metal bones. Sparks convulse from an artificial eye as my foe drops his pistol and falls onto his back, motionless. I re-collect the handbag and wallet, jump into the vehicle, and Anguson U-turns as I check my bleeding forearm.

'You see that shit? Fucking cyborg,' I say as the pain intensifies.

'Metal face – a lot of underground fighters are getting them. That's why I had to go through a metal detector before my championship fights,' Anguson says.

'What about the way he jumped? Must've been cybernetic legs, too. How much of his body was even human?' I say.

'Enough for you to kill him.'

Blood streams from my forearm as Anguson races to the capsule hotel, straight through a red light, and I am not wearing a seatbelt. I grip the wound tight and try to wriggle my fingers, but intense pain spreads to my shoulder, straining every arm muscle. The haul on my lap had better make the injury worthwhile.

'Shit, you've been shot,' Anguson raises his voice over the radio music.

'No... shit...' I grimace as blood consumes my hand and I swear the bullet is lodged on a nerve. Agony tempts me to release the pressure, but I cannot risk bleeding out in a getaway car.

'Does it hurt?'

'What do you think?' I splutter through my clenched teeth, gasping.

'You shot anywhere else?'

'I-I don't think so.' I glance at my uninjured legs and torso. 'The blood is ruining this lovely shirt, though.' A laugh is quickly replaced by a whimper and tears so I hold my breath, trembling.

'Just as well. It's not like we can stroll into a hospital. Let's get to the hotel room and patch you up... Oh fuck!'

Looking up from my gun wound, I see a police car coming in the opposite direction with blue lights flashing. Anguson drives calmly towards a roundabout, but as we pass, the cops glare suspiciously, then the passenger cop leans forwards. Two beeps are followed by a siren as the police car skids on the three-lane road, turning into our lane. *'Drive!'* Anguson floors the accelerator, racing over the roundabout island and away from the city centre with the police car in pursuit.

Anguson swerves onto the path as two workers pull bins across the road to their garbage truck. We grind against a wall and return to the road, swerving around bend after bend, and churning up turf as we cross a school field.

'Don't just sit there! Fucking shoot them before backup arrives,' Anguson roars.

Leaning out the window, I bounce and jerk, unable to steady myself with my injured arm as I unload my KAL 10. Bullet holes appear in the bonnet of the police car and then its windscreen shatters. The passenger cop slumps in his seat, but the driver is unhurt, and he turns his vehicle away from the line of fire.

'They've given up the chase, but keep an eye out for their friends,' I say.

We escape the school field, sideswiping a parked vehicle as we bounce onto a narrow road. I change clips as two more police cars emerge at the bottom of the street; their sirens loud enough to wake every nearby resident. I spray fire, but the jerking of the vehicle and distance to the target affects my aim and a window shatters on a terraced house.

A shadowy figure stands in the road, staring, and we head straight for what appears to be a catatonic woman. She raises her arm and bends her hand down, and two flashes from her wrist are accompanied by two bangs.

Our front tyres explode and the rims grind the road as the figure shines in our headlights, naked and metallic.

'That's no girl, it's a fucking droid!'

Anguson ducks and I shoot the droid's gun-arm which twitches and sparks as I change clips. Glowing blue eyes glance at bullet damage on the droid's shell and then stare at our road-grinding motorcar. The droid jumps onto our windscreen, shattering the glass with a punch from its functioning arm. I unload a clip into its face and chest, tearing away its silver/blue shell to reveal mechanical parts.

Anguson slams on the brakes and the combat droid flies onto the road, tumbling violently. Our vehicle goes straight over its body with a judder and in the rear-view mirror, I see our foe faltering on a broken leg. A pursuing police car smashes into the droid and a mass of sparking metal flies through the air.

'What the fuck are the police doing with combat droids?' Anguson asks as I brush fragments of glass from my injured forearm.

'No idea. I was under the impression the human-like models were unreliable and too costly with the technology being so new,' I say.

'There could be more in the area and I'm guessing our image will have been shared across the police network,' Anguson says.

'Let's get off-road and hide before this thing catches fire.'

Reaching from the window, I spray bullets at the pursuing cars as Anguson drives along a pavement between terraces. Our vehicle judders and dips with a bang and the screeching loudens. 'Shit, that's the third tyre.' Anguson crosses a narrow road, mounts a kerb onto grass, and crashes through a temporary fence fixed into small blocks. I shove the stolen wallet and purse into my pockets and look up to see a vague rollercoaster track.

Anguson and I exit the one-tyred motorcar beside a stall and run through a funfair in twilight. 'I don't think anyone followed us,' Anguson gasps as we slow near a merry-go-round with saddled seahorses and dolphins. The greyness of the attractions increases the tension, kind of like an old black and white movie.

'Wait, I hear a noise,' I whisper and we crouch with KAL 10's in hand, peering around the funfair for signs of movement. I climb onto the base of the merry-go-round, sneaking between poles and sea creatures to the other side. Partially concealed by a dolphin, I scan our moonlit surroundings but see nothing other than stationary rides.

I return to Anguson and shrug, but then I hear a noise and raise my eyebrows. 'I definitely heard that one. Let's hide in *there*.' Anguson points to a ghost train and we hop over a fence at the queuing area, sneaking through a skull mouth into a dark tunnel. 'What ya think it was? An animal? A droid? Police?'

'If it was police, I reckon we would've heard their engines, their voices. Probably just an animal,' I say as we follow the track past obscure railcarts.

'When we were running, I wouldn't have noticed a sound, the way I was gasping. Maybe the police were cruising by and spotted the vehicle,' Anguson says.

'In that case, we'd be better off hiding in here until the funfair opens, then blend into the crowd,' I say.

'The way you're dressed, you won't be blending into any crowd.' Anguson sniggers.

'*Funny.*'

Green lights suddenly reveal the interior of the ghost train with a ghoulish cackling. 'What the hell?' I say as chains rattle on fake stone walls covered with giant cobwebs and squirming spiders. I glance back to the tunnel mouth, but see no sign of human presence beyond the railcarts.

'Maybe it's the staff arriving early,' Anguson whispers.

'Or maybe it's the cops ensuring they can see what they're doing. Get your gun ready and walk back-to-back,' I say.

Anguson takes rear-guard as we pass a corpse on a rocking chair behind iron bars. I flinch as we turn a corner to see a one-eyed monster severed in half, standing on its hands. Passing skulls on the floor, I spot a skeleton with red eyes and chattering teeth, and I feel like a five-year-old child. This shit is scaring the crap out of me.

My legs buckle and I slide down Anguson's back as a figure lunges out of the shadows. I shoot a werewolf with purple fur until its body is reduced to pieces of polystyrene. Anguson spins on the track and mutters: 'Fuck's sake, compose yourself.'

Getting to my feet, I approach a zombie with a bloody mouth, and an indistinct figure jumps from an archway. I chuckle as a cyclops raises its arm, but then I drop to the floor because a flashing light reveals a combat droid. It fires a pulse of energy and Anguson falls onto my back, knocking the air from my lungs. The agony causes my eyeballs to bulge as I squeeze the trigger and sparks fly from holes in the droid's shell.

I push the motionless Anguson onto his side and approach the combat droid, staring at its punctured blue and silver panels, its narrow waist and feminine hips, its angular nose and lips, and its glowing blue eyes which fade to grey. The combat droid seems fully deactivated so I save my ammunition, walking backwards past the waving zombie. I crouch and notice Anguson is still breathing – good job the combat droid's pulse phaser was set to stun.

It will likely take Anguson minutes to regain consciousness so I check the ghost train for further enemies. A vampire lunges against my shoulder and I shrug it off, firing as I spot human-like movement. A policeman falls face-down on the track; his blood almost white as it reflects a flashing light. I hear yelling so I sneak from the track into a passage of fake stone walls.

I feel my way through the passage to a sliver of light, unlocking a bolt and emerging outside at sunrise. Crossing open ground, I encircle a merry-go-round and shoot cops situated at each end of the tunnel. The children will get a real scare when they visit the ghost train in the morning.

I run to a pirate ship, climb inside and use the vantage of the stern and then the bow to scan for further cops. One sneaks towards the ghost train so I shred his shoulders and he face-plants the ground. Hearing gunfire, I duck and scurry away from the pirate ship, dashing towards the merry-go-round. I lie flat and crawl beneath the base, wincing as my injured forearm meets dead grass.

At the other end of the merry-go-round, I glimpse leather shoes and shoot until I sever a foot – the resulting scream sounds inhuman. I change clips as the cop twitches on the ground and his eyes widen when he spots my KAL 10. Bullets remove the flesh from his face as I empty my clip, switching to my last. Shit.

Seeing no further shoes, I scramble from the cover of the merry-go-round, running through the funfair and hiding inside a dodgem car. A combat droid leaps from a rollercoaster track and as it lands on the grass, I spray fire from its metal legs to its gun-arm.

The combat droid raises its sparking gun-arm which does not respond, but neither does my KAL 10. My foe clumsily charges in my direction; its damaged left leg buckling as I spin on the damp grass. I dash for the ghost train to retrieve Anguson who is hopefully ready to awaken, but I fall as I am struck in the coccyx.

The combat droid wraps its forearm around my throat and loose wiring provides a small electric shock. It mutters gibberish, probably reading my rights as Anguson emerges from the skull mouth, hurdles the queuing fence, and flying-kicks its metal head. The two of us yank its forearm and our combined strength is enough to free my neck. My rescuer unloads a full clip, rendering our foe inactive as I regain my breath.

Anguson approaches a dead cop at the ghost train and retrieves keys from his pocket. We exit the funfair by hurdling the temporary fence and then we steal one of the parked police cars. Oh, the joy.

BACK IN STYLE

HEARING RADIO CHATTER, I glance around the matte black interior of the police car – the touchscreen on the dashboard, the gadgetry between our leather seats, the guns mounted in the door likely to have fingerprint recognition. I am tempted to switch on the siren, but this is no time for fun and games. We are officially cop killers.

'We should hit a maglev highway and fly to the next city,' Anguson suggests.

'I'd rather minimise my time in this thing in case we're tracked. We just destroyed three combat droids, for fuck's sake. The police will have our pictures and I lost count of the number of their friends we killed,' I say and my heart pounds as the full extent of our predicament dawns.

'Yeah, something tells me they won't be taking us in for questioning. They'll want blood,' Anguson says.

'And who can blame them? I've never been a fan of the police, but I never wanted to kill the fuckers.'

'It's no different from the military, Leo. Men are forced into positions they don't want to be in. We're good guys in a bad situation, that's all.'

'Good guys? I'm not so sure about that.' My eyes burn as I spot a shopping complex several miles from the murder scene. 'Perfect place to seek medical treatment. Let's park up and find a chemist.'

Anguson parks in a residential street, ensuring the police car is out of sight of traffic on the main road. We walk to the shopping complex, entering a fenced carpark which has an allotment of rusty sheds at the far end. The buildings in the complex are white with stone rosettes on the walls, and all are closed with the exception of a large supermarket. Above the arching doorway, an electronic board shows an orange doll's face with a dripping paint effect. The display switches to a giant doughnut with icing and sprinkles.

'You'd better go in. My bullet wound will draw attention. Try to get the following – a First Aid kit, antiseptic cream, tweezers, a needle and thread, hair dye, razors, scissors, and new clothes. Oh, and some food. You got all that?'

'Er, kind'a,' Anguson says.

'Be quick, the cop car might have a tracker,' I say and Anguson marches below the arching entrance of the supermarket.

As I stand with crossed arms to hide my gun wound, the carpark gradually fills, shutters roll up on stores, and sleepy customers pass through the doors. A staff member cleans tables with white and green umbrellas which are standing within a rope fence.

Anguson returns to the carpark with shopping bags and we wander into the streets of Batavia. The sun grows increasingly hot and rush hour traffic turns the air toxic as we bicker about the correct direction. We head towards the glass towers until the streets become familiar and civilians swarm the pavements. The sun is high in the pink sky as we finally reach the capsule hotel.

Inside our cosy 'room', I inspect my purple forearm which has an entry wound, but not an exit wound. This comes as no surprise because it feels like the bullet is pressing against my radius. 'Shit, I forgot about painkillers.' I poke the hole with tweezers as my eyes water and my clammy hand trembles.

Prying my flesh, I glimpse a red lump among fat cells and sinews which I twice prod. The surface seems metallic so I grasp the sides, hyperventilating as I remove a tiny bullet which feels massive. Blood again soaks into the bed sheets as I slide the bullet into my pocket. I squeeze antiseptic cream into the wound and grab a large sticking plaster and a bandage.

'You sure you don't wanna stitch the wound, first?' Anguson says.

'If I feel any more pain, I swear I'll fucking pass out,' I say.

'You seriously putting a sticking plaster over a bullet wound?' Anguson smirks.

'*Yes*.' I place the plaster over the sticky red hole and then wrap the bandage tight.

'Right, time for a makeover.' I remove our new electric razor from the packaging, plug it into a wall socket, and shave my frizzy beard which has grown so long that I repeatedly clog and unclog the razor. The buzzing makes my face tingle and when I finish, I stroke my smooth cheeks, eager to see my ugly reflection.

'I have an idea.' Anguson smirks, picking up the electric razor and flicking off the trapped hair. He switches the power on and moves the buzzing blades towards my microphone head.

'Oh no.' I hold up my palm.

'Just trust me. What's the worst that could happen?'

Anguson shaves my head, nicking my ears and leaving the blanket covered with matted hair as well as congealing blood. What the hell are the hotel staff going to think? I touch my head which is now bald on either side, but unshaven in the middle.

'What the fuck have you done?' I mutter.

'Mohawk.' Anguson removes a plastic tub from one of the carrier bags. 'I even got you some styling gel.' Anguson unscrews the lid, rubs the gel in his hands and applies it to my hair, sniggering.

'I'm gonna have to check this out in the mirror.'

Grabbing my new clothes and some shower gel, I head to the men's room and face a mirror over the sink. Small red spots cover my skin which has patches of stubble missed by the razor. My thick lips are chapped, my eyes are puffy, and my frizzy mohawk is shining.

I take a hot shower, careful not to wet my bandage, and the styling gel runs from my hair, burning my eyes. I emerge minty-fresh but feeling like crap – exhausted, stressed, head aching, arm and feet ready to fall off. I get dressed in black jeans, a red top with an eagle emblem, and brown leather shoes that would make me resemble a regular person if not for my mohawk.

Returning to the capsule, I apply antiseptic cream to my itchy feet which have hard, navy patches – this does not look good. I put on my socks and shoes, remove the messy quilt cover, fold it up, and place it in the corner, then I devour a doughnut.

Minutes later, Anguson climbs into the capsule with a fresh outfit, a bald head and bushy, ginger beard. 'I see you bought the hair dye.' I point my finger, unable to contain my laughter, but Anguson just shrugs and puts his bag in the corner. We place our notes on the bed and count a total of three thousand, five hundred and ninety seven remins.

'We're almost there,' Anguson says.

'Well, best purchase some more ammo, I'm out.' I slouch against the wall, reluctant to leave the capsule, and my mouth opens to speak, but only a sigh emerges.

'As soon as we've eaten… I'm starving.' Anguson delves into a carrier bag for a donut. 'A bite to eat and then it's back to action. Hopefully, we can keep the collateral damage to a minimum.'

'This entire thing is getting more surreal by the minute. Here we are, shortly after a mass-killing in a funfair, all too casual about doing this shit again.' I collect the bag from Anguson's grasp and reach inside, removing a packet of crisps.

'I'd rather you were casual than a crying baby.' Anguson spits crumbs as he speaks. 'Anyways, who the fuck are you kidding? Remorse has clearly affected you. And you haven't stopped whining about that bullet wound.'

I pause in silence, staring at my bandaged forearm, then I retrieve the blood-encrusted bullet from my dirty shorts and roll it in my palm. For some reason, I feel attached to a piece of metal which could have ended my life, like it would make a nice keepsake – a reminder of my mortality.

Scenes of our many gun fights replay before my eyes, thousands of bullets that came our way, and not one was able to kill us. Shit, this was the only bullet that even came close.

'What about those combat droids, though? Sure, they don't have a mech's armour or firepower, but they're fast, agile, and human-like,' Anguson says.

'Should that not be superhuman-like?' I slot the bullet into my trouser pocket.

'Like cyborgs without the fleshy parts. If they come from Nyberu, this war could get very interesting,' Anguson says.

'Be damn expensive to fight a war with combat droids, though. Anyways, they probably originated in Anatolia. Atheon Tech tested something similar in Adyla a few years back. The problem was the droids were bad at distinguishing the good guys from the bad guys,' I say.

'Maybe that's why they toned down the firepower. Just as well or we'd be fucking dead,' Anguson says.

'We should be fucking dead, given the amount of shit we've faced. I'm not a spiritual man, but I sometimes wonder whether fate is looking out for us,' I say.

'There's only one thing looking out for us – and that's each other,' Anguson says.

We eat junk food, covering the bed in crumbs and wrappers in addition to the hair and blood, and then we leave the capsule hotel. Our robbery outfits are scrunched inside a carrier bag which we dump into a bin, several blocks away. We return to the arms dealer, purchase ammunition, and enter an alley where I slot clips into my machine pistol and chest holster, just to be prepared.

As we pass a pallet standing against freshly-painted graffiti, we pause in response to the sound of crying. Anguson and I peer between garbage cans to see a scantily-clad girl sitting on the ground, hunched among buzzing flies. Her face is buried into her forearms which are resting on her knees.

'What are you doing down there?' Anguson asks; the brute suddenly gentle in his tone.

'I'm all alone,' the girl says with the sweetest, most innocent voice.

'I can see that. Is there anything I can do to help?' Anguson crouches, holds out his hand and hesitates.

'H-help... Can I come with you?' The girl looks upwards, flicking her blue hair to reveal a peach complexion and large, sapphire eyes which are not quite natural. As she flutters her long eyelashes, a bluebottle lands on her nose, but she, or rather *it* does not flinch.

'Leave it, it's just a discarded pleasure droid.' I turn away, feeling weird about referring to a humanoid as *it*. 'There must be a problem with... it.'

'How do you know she's a pleasure droid?' Anguson says.

'Pretty, emotional, highly realistic, but not quite right,' I say.

'Then why didn't they switch her off?' Anguson says.

'I think my owner forgot to remove my power supply.' The pleasure droid whispers as artificial tears pour. 'He threw me out in a temper. He said I'm not functioning correctly... I just want to please.'

'Not functioning correctly? I'm guessing power surge. I've heard of these things tearing cocks off in their excitement. This is why no-one uses them back in Anatolia. Too fucking dangerous,' I say.

'If you take me with you, I can show you the Anatolian establishment south of the river where I stayed before I was sold on. I think you'd like it. Most men do. It's a gambling den, whorehouse, inn. It contains all the things men seem to enjoy.'

'Well, we do need a place to stay. Can't stay in the capsule hotel forever.' I scratch my chin, then swat flies away from my face.

'Do you have a name?' Anguson says.

'My name is July Cummings.' The pleasure droid proudly stands to shake Anguson's hand, then she reaches for mine, but I ignore the gesture.

'Well, July, I'm Sydney and this is Leo.' Anguson grins with eyes dilated by his lust for a robot in a junkheap.

'Oh, we're using our Sunday names now?' I sneer.

The pleasure droid leads from the alley, past the giant statue of Ceros, and down an embankment aligned with office buildings. Sparkly blue short-shorts reveal slender, luscious pins and an arse with a natural wriggle. And from this angle, July seems to be one hundred percent human.

We come to a river, crossing a semi-circular swing-bridge which curves outwards, attached to an arch by cables. Halfway across, we stop to take in the view of modern apartment blocks, crumbling mills, cranes carrying girders, and tied-up fishing boats. Below our feet, white fences stand in the river to direct boats into the correct position.

'July, you look kind'a familiar. Are you modelled on a real person by any chance?' Anguson says.

'Yes, my body was modelled on adult actress Jane Apolinario and I've been programmed with all of her techniques.'

'Fuck me, I've hit the fucking jackpot.' Anguson grins and pinches the pleasure droid's arse. 'Ooh!' She jumps and puts her fingers over her lips, then fixes Anguson's gaze as though she has an official new owner.

'Fucking creepy... Well, not as creepy as the ones modelled on celebrities without permission. Those mosquito cams get everywhere,' I say.

'If you don't put a detector in your dressing room, you deserve what you get, I reckon. I heard about a droid modelled on my ex-girlfriend Navah Lakin. I was tempted to buy one to confuse the paps and piss her off!'

Anguson laughs, glancing to July who rests her elbows on the side-railing near a gull.

'So tell me, what are you doing in Batavia? Anatolians are an infrequent sight, nowadays,' July says.

'We're, er, workers. Been here a while, but we're gonna be leaving pretty soon,' Anguson says.

'You do know it's not interested in small talk?' I inhale a fishy odour carried by the breeze. 'It's just programmed to keep you company.'

'How did you hurt your arm?' July stares at my denim sleeve which has fully covered my bandage. I hesitate as a family walk past, in the unlikely event they can understand our conversation.

'How did you know I hurt my arm?' I whisper through the corner of my mouth.

'I can tell from the movement; it's stiff and unnatural. Also, your hand is discoloured,' July says.

'It was a work accident.' I stand straight, curling my lips and watching the clouds which are not sufficient to block the warmth of the sun.

'Is that why you're not working today?' July says.

'Yeah, let's just say we're seeking alternative employment,' I say.

'Maybe you could work as doormen. Fellas your size would be perfect,' July says as drizzle creates ripples among the rubbish in the river.

'Only problem is, we're not exactly fluent in Nusantaran. Makes job-seeking difficult,' Anguson says.

'Oh, I can help you there. I'm fluent in–'

'One hundred and seventy nine languages,' I interrupt.

'Yes, how did you know?' July says.

'Just a lucky guess.' I remove the bullet from my pocket, spit and wipe the blood to reveal its shiny surface. Although it would make a nice keepsake, I should eradicate evidence so I toss it into the red-tinged water. 'Let's go.'

July leads over the swing-bridge into a dark and decrepit corner of town where brick and sandstone are soot-covered, door signs are rotting, fly posters are numerous, and people are scowling, belching, spitting. As we follow the narrow street, we pass a window display of dragons and skulls which look like tattoo designs. And I had better keep Anguson away before he splurges our cash redecorating his skin.

At the next grimy building, July points to a red sign with golden lettering that is actually readable: *The Swine Inn.*

'I take it this is our destination,' I mutter.

THE SWINE INN

JULY LEADS US INTO A BAR where the curtains are drawn and amber lights illuminate burgundy wallpaper and golden beer taps. A dart board and pool table are visible beyond a wooden partition with clouded windows bearing The Swine Inn logo. Twenty or so patrons are sitting at the bar and tables, some quiet and miserable, others boisterous and jovial. A barman, with a goatee and white shirt, looks up as he dries a glass with a towel.

'Two pints of Brown Ale, please,' I say and the barman pulls two pints as July sits on a stool.

'That'll be three remins, forty, please.'

'That's a damn sight cheaper than back home.' I hand over the money and we collect our glasses.

'Certainly is… So what brings you into this fine establishment? It's not often we see unfamiliar faces during the day, what with the war and everything.'

'Our contract in Sununate just ended and there wasn't much work about so we thought we'd come to Batavia, try our luck. We need a room if you've got any going,' I say.

'Sure, our rooms are twenty five remins a night.'

'Twenty five remins? That's half the price of the bloody capsule hotel.' Anguson chokes on his drink.

'Don't tell me you were staying at the Men Teng.' The barman chuckles. 'They inflate the price because they know gullible tourists will pay over the odds.'

'You seriously mean I've been paying extra to share a fucking capsule with this stinking oaf?' Anguson says and we exchange frowns as the barman howls with laughter.

'Y-you been sharing a capsule?' The barman points a finger and holds his belly. 'Must've been cosy.'

'We'll take two rooms, please. Leslie can share with his *lady friend*. I could do with some privacy,' I say and Anguson glares in response to my use of his secret middle-name.

'Two seconds, I'll get the keys and the forms.' The barman disappears through a doorway between wine racks and returns a little over two seconds later. 'If each of you could fill in your details and sign at the bottom.' Anguson and I complete the forms without reading the fine print and the barman gives us our keys. 'The rooms are through *that* doorway and up the stairs.'

In the opposite direction to which the barman pointed, a man walks through a door with a stained-glass window. Music becomes audible as a semi-clad girl dances in darkness and a wrinkly hand touches her waist. Beyond the mismatched pair, I glimpse swaying silhouettes and then I hear shrieking laughter.

'What's through *there*?' I point across the bar to the doorway.

'Oh, that's the entertainment room. I'm sure you'll enjoy it,' the barman says.

'Come on, Leslie, let's take a look.'

We pass through the door with the stained-glass window, entering a disco with swirling lights and nineties dance-music my dad used to listen to. Men fatter and uglier than me are drinking and dancing with girls as pretty and artificial as July. Anguson and I stand at the bar, admiring the cleavages on display and ordering a second round of beers.

'Don't you think it's a little rude bringing a pleasure droid into a whorehouse?' an ageing barman asks.

'July here is a paying guest – the wife of my friend Leslie. And you wouldn't have had three new customers, if not for her suggesting this place,' I say.

'Your friend's wife looks strangely familiar… Well, Mr er–'

'Jardine.'

'If you would like a *wife* for this evening,' the barman waves a scantily-clad group over from a table, 'you can choose from this bunch. We have the girls here – Tara, Tosha, Kelly, Steph. And the boys – Colin, Graham, Jon, and Zach. Or if you would like something of the hermaphrodite variety, we have Erica and Craig. I'm not here to judge. Each pleasure droid is five remins per hour.'

'Just get me another beer, please.' I gulp the second beer down in record time and wipe my mouth with my wrist. The pleasure droids pout and flutter their eyelashes as their sequinned outfits reflect the disco lights, but I turn my shoulder. Froth dribbles from the brim as I collect my pint and slide my empty glass to the barman.

We have found the perfect place for help to return home, but we have also found the perfect place to avoid returning home. Staying here means we do not have to worry about conscription and we could have plenty of fun.

'While you're getting drunk, I think I'll show July to our room,' Anguson says as I place my pint on a beer mat and the barman vanishes through a door.

'You're going to fuck her, aren't you?' Anguson remains silent. 'You are, aren't you?' Anguson downs his pint and leads July towards the door with the stained glass window. 'If she malfunctions, she'll tear your fucking cock off, idiot.'

I drink my beer alone, watching a chubby man chewing the face of a beautiful droid with silver hair. And I cannot see the appeal of kissing rubber lips, no matter how plump, shiny, and luscious they are... Actually, who the fuck am I kidding?

'So, what's your story?' a voice asks and I turn to see the ageing barman has returned. His shiny bald patch and confident tone suggest he could be the landlord.

'Work in construction. A job just ended so I'm looking for something else. Thought I'd take a few days off and relax first, though,' I say.

'You another one of those ex-military types?' The barman leans on his elbows and a smile spreads to his bloodshot cheeks.

'Nah, just a regular guy. You get many of those ex-military types in here?' I say.

'About the only guests we have these days – runaways. Can't return home, afraid to go to Nyberu in case they get arrested so they come to the closest thing to neutral territory. Not that it'll remain neutral much longer.'

'Yeah, I've heard that. I just don't get why any nation would join a war with no possible winners,' I say.

'Nusantara have tried to stay out of the war, but it's becoming increasingly apparent Anatolia will spare no-one if Nyberu falls. The only reason they haven't vaporised every city is because the other side can do the same to them.'

'But more than a few cities *have* been vaporised,' I say.

'So far, warheads have been dropped in moments of anger or desperation, but retaliation makes them fear escalation; mutual destruction is no good to anyone. There's a race going on to take down subs, satellites, bases; remove the other side's doomsday capability. First side to succeed, wins the war. And Anatolia has better technology, more money, lower morals. They'll stop at nothing because their fucking Goddess *wants* them to win.'

'Yeah, our people are real bastards. I've been thinking about returning home, but when you put it like that, it doesn't seem such an appealing option,' I say.

'Between you and me, it may actually be better if Anatolia loses. Not that the other side is so wonderful.'

'Personally, I just want people to stop fucking dying.' I drink the froth in the bottom of my glass.

'I'll drink to that, Mr Jardine. Name's James Jones – the owner of this fine establishment.' James raises a pint glass, nods, and drinks his beer.

HANGOVER FROM HELL

WAKING NAKED WITH A HANGOVER, I turn to see a pretty face and pink nipples pointing towards the ceiling and I adopt a wide grin. I stroke the belly of the companion I have no memory of meeting, glancing down her lithe body to see a... fucking humongous cock! Heart pounding, I scramble out of bed, tangled in the blanket, and I bump my head against the wall.

'Morning handsome, something startle you?' She, or he, or it, flicks their long black hair from their cheek.

'Y-you're... What the fuck are you?'

'A little speciality for a man with unique taste.'

'You're one of those pleasure droids, aren't you? Fuck, I must've been drunk. Can't remember a damn thing. Quick, get your clothes on and get out before Anguson sees.'

'I'm afraid you must settle your bill first. Eleven hours of pleasure is one hundred and ten remins.'

'Eleven hours? I spent the entire night sleeping.'

'Not the entire night, just eight hours, and you're the one who insisted I stay and cuddle.'

'Stop it, *please*, I think I'm gonna vomit.'

'Oh, stop being melodramatic. Your kinky little secrets are safe with me.' The pleasure droid touches its lips to stifle a giggle.

I glance around the room of peach decor, seeing scattered clothes, and I locate my trousers strewn across a tasselled lampshade and dresser. I remove my wallet from my pocket, count the money, and hand it to the pleasure droid which smiles; its pert titties provoke a semi until I think of what lies below. Seriously, how can something so pretty have such a humongous cock? This is a sick joke.

The pleasure droid picks its sparkly clothes from the floor and gets dressed, then attempts to kiss my cheek but I pull away. 'Until next time, handsome.' *It* leaves the bedroom and I sit naked, clutching my head as pain intensifies in my brain and forearm. Shit, I remember what happened now – I was shot by a pimp.

I get dressed in last night's smelly clothes and venture into town to purchase painkillers from a chemist. As I browse the shelves, most of the labels are gibberish, but one appears to resemble Eurofyn, a popular Anatolian painkiller. I buy two boxes and swallow three pills in the hope I have chosen the correct product.

The pain in my forearm mercifully eases as I return to the Men Teng capsule hotel to collect our belongings. Our 'room' still bears the stench of trenchfoot, despite the fresh bed sheets, and I pity the hotel staff who cleaned our mess. Our clothing, towels, electric shaver, and medical supplies are stuffed into carrier bags in the corner.

I log into the compuscreen and run an internet search, finding a website with an image of oily black toes. I shudder at the thought mine could be heading in the same direction. The text below the image reads:

Trench foot is an immersion foot syndrome caused by prolonged exposure to cold, damp, and unsanitary conditions. It takes its name from trench warfare in which the condition was commonplace.

It can lead to cyanosis (skin turning blue) due to lack of blood supply. A strong odour is an indication that necrosis (tissue death) is setting in. If left untreated, trench foot is likely to result in gangrene and foot loss, or even death. However, if treated early enough, full recovery is possible, although the healing process can lead to severe pain.

If affected, it is important to ensure feet are kept clean, warm, and dry for a period of six months to aid recovery. If the symptoms worsen, medical treatment is urgently required to clear any infection and repair the cell damage. Once the cell damage becomes extensive, it is usually irreparable and amputation is then the only option.

Shuddering, I dash to the shower and vigorously scrub and dry my itchy, blue soles. I apply antiseptic cream to my bullet wound and feet, and then I change into clean but ridiculous clothes. I check out of the hotel, handing the key into reception without talking, and I collect our deposit. Presumably, the cost of last night was deducted from the figure.

Upon return to The Swine Inn, I disregard the barman's greeting, due to my shame, and hurry to my bedroom. The lack of compuscreen or any form of entertainment means I just stare out of the bay window. Beyond a packed carpark lies a pleasant parkland with blossoming trees and swans in a large pond. Someone knocks at the door, but I ignore the caller, enjoying the warmth of sunlight on my face. The knocking continues and I know it can only be the oaf. Please say he does not know.

I open the door a little and a shirtless Anguson barges into my bedroom, knocking me back and spreading his arms wide. July follows him inside and he smacks her arse, causing her to jump and say: 'Ooh!'

'I see you changed your mind on the pleasure droids,' Anguson says.

'I've no idea what you're talking about,' I mumble, turning away to see the oaf grinning in the dresser mirror.

'Who the fuck you kidding?' Anguson booms. 'It appears you had even more fun than I did, the noise you were making, but at least I didn't pay *That* would be sad.'

'Please stop. This hangover's killing me.' I breathe heavily through my nose. 'By the way, I collected your clothes from the hotel. They're in a bag in the corner.'

'I'll get them later. Let's go downstairs and relax. They've gotta football game on the big screen,' Anguson says.

'Fine, but I'm on soft drinks,' I say.

Heading downstairs, we sit in the front bar with July, watching the Medio Magpies take on bitter rivals the Abana Black Cats on the big screen. Footballers, of course, are too important to send to war.

Shalan Aerer scores a goal from outside the box, and Anguson and I rise to our feet, spilling our pints as we roar. The men sitting at the next table glare, presumably Black Cats supporters. Aerer scores two more goals, leading the Magpies to a comfortable three-nil win which eases my hangover no end.

After the match analysis, an Anatolian state-sponsored news broadcast comes on, and the newsreader has fury in her eyes:

'Due to sickening human rights violations committed by Nyberu, including the deliberate poisoning of water supplies, and the launching of thermonuclear warheads which were thankfully intercepted, the Anatolian air-force have been forced to take decisive action.

'The Nyberun city of Lakashina and surrounding towns have been vaporised by an anti-matter bomb. This move has destroyed key weapons manufacturing facilities as well as a large military installation, and will significantly impact the Nyberun economy. The loss of civilian life is most regrettable, but this is a fight for survival, for freedom and justice, and it is a fight Anatolia will win.'

'Those bastards. Nyberu hasn't bombed civilians in months and has only ever done so in retaliation to our strikes. I'd be willing to bet San Teria poisoned their own water supply as a fucking excuse,' James Jones, the owner, booms from over the bar.

'You really think they're *that* evil?' I say, even though I share the sentiment, because I want to establish who I am dealing with before I open up.

'That evil and a whole lot more. Everyone in here, who has served on the front-line, understands. Apparently, for every antimatter bomb detonated, there are two that are intercepted.'

'Yeah, that's why soldiers have been defecting. If it comes down to it, I'm prepared to fight for Nusantara before those San Terian bastards destroy the world,' a man in a yellow shirt yells from a crowded table.

'Fight for Nusantara? Against our own men?' a short man with a red cap replies from the neighbouring table.

'Our own men are on the wrong side. Their lives are worth no more than Nusantaran lives, Nyberun lives, Lamantian lives... If you have San Terian sympathies, you're in the wrong place,' the man in a yellow shirt says.

'San Terian sympathies, you kidding me?' The man in the red cap sniffs.

'Hey, no-one below Level Two Citizenship has San Terian sympathies,' I interrupt, attempting to diffuse the tension.

'And rightfully so.' The man in a yellow shirt stares in our direction; the skin around his eyes crinkling suspiciously. 'Hey, you look familiar. Don't I–'

'Yeah, yeah, he looks like cage-fighter Sydney Anguson, gets it all the time.' I glance to Anguson who has July on his lap on the next bar stool, and both are grinning, oblivious to the conversation.

'Not him, *you*.' The man rises from his seat and leans forwards to gain a closer look, pursing his lips, like a cop eyeing a suspect.

'I'm not Sydney Anguson either!' I laugh.

'You from Fort Edwin by any chance?'

'No, Medio,' I say.

'You sure you're not ex-military?'

'Haven't had the pleasure of conscription so far.' I swig my beer and the man in a yellow shirt frowns as though he knows my words are untruthful, as though we have previously crossed paths, but his face is unfamiliar.

A younger man interrupts: 'I'm from Medio too. Name's Asias.'

The younger man approaches our table, places his pint on a mat and shakes my hand with a firm grip. Although not too tall, he appears to be strong for his age with broad-shoulders and an athletic physique. His square face is unblemished, as brown as mine, and his stare lingers, sad, angry, confused, amiable, all at once. I recognise instantly the scars of the battlefield, the agony of lost souls burnt into *his* soul. There is no mistaking Asias is military – a younger version of me.

'Don't get any Magpies fans in here. Good to find some allies, at last.' Asias glances to Anguson who is still canoodling with July, and then he returns his gaze to me. 'I heard you work in construction, me too. I might be able to get you some work.'

'That'd be good, Asias, if you can. The name's Leo Jardine.'

'Good to meet you, Leo, I'll see what I can do,' Asias says.

'So how'd a young lad like you end up in Batavia?' I finish my beer and gesture to James Jones who gives a thumbs up and pulls a pint.

'Ex-military, just another runaway, took a boat ride from Nyberu. So many were shot in my first few weeks on the front line, I couldn't take it. I saw my friends stepping on land mines, crawling in the mud with no legs.

It's only luck that I didn't step on one, too. But the worst thing was the killing – young men like me, innocent civilians, *kids*. It's hard to take, ya know.'

'Yeah, no-one should be exposed to war, especially not kids,' I say.

'You can say that again. I have a baby back home – *Arturo*. I was sent away not long after he was born. The worst thing about it is, I wasn't a conscript, I signed up. I can't believe how stupid I was.'

James Jones brings my pint so I give him two remins and he collects my empty glass, stacking it with the others beside the washer.

'Wow, there are dumb decisions and then there are *dumb* decisions,' I say as James brings my change of thirty *somethings* – I have no idea what Nusantarans call their smaller coins.

'I had grand ideas of being all heroic, winning the war quickly, making the world a safer place, even earning promotion. I just wanted to provide for my boy. Being a bottom-leveller's a struggle, but I didn't realise Level Three Citizenship would make me disposable.'

'You really are naive. They'll say anything to get you to sign up to Level Three Citizenship. As soon as you do, you're their property.' I pause to scratch my chin. 'I was smart enough to leave before the conscription letter arrived.'

'Since I left, I haven't told my woman. I'm too ashamed to admit I was wrong about everything, that I couldn't handle military life, that I'm a traitor. If I return before the war is over, I'll be shot for cowardice. My only chance of seeing my son again is if the Lamantian alliance wins the war, but that may mean joining the Nusantaran army – more fighting.'

'So your woman thinks you're still on the front line?' I say.

'No idea, I fled the battlefield with a few friends. Our superiors probably assumed we were blown up. Ortellia may well have been told I'm dead. It's such a fucking mess.'

Asias and I turn sharply in response to roaring as a man's shirt is soaked by beer. 'You'll pay for that, you stupid bastard!' Two sneering brutes rise from their seats to square off and they seem in no mood for reconciliation. The wet man punches the other in the jaw, and he staggers into an occupied chair, then the pair lock arms around necks.

James Jones leaves his bar and prowls towards the struggle, growling, 'If you want to fight, you can continue this outside,' but the men ignore the instruction. One bashes into a table, spilling drinks, so Anguson and I rise from our seats, grabbing their arms and removing the pair from the establishment.

Anguson and I dump the brawlers onto the pavement; my one functioning hand enough to restrain a bloody-lipped drunk. Girls, or possibly lady-boys, cross the road in high-heels as their quarrel is resumed, and we return to The Swine Inn, no longer concerned. The pair can tear each other to pieces for all I care.

We take our seats next to July, sip our pints of Brown Ale, and James Jones approaches from behind the bar.

'Thanks for that, men. Things have been pretty rowdy in here, recently, especially during football games and between the hours of ten and two. I could do with someone working the doors and you guys would be perfect. Even the toughest ex-military wouldn't argue with either of you. If you're looking for work, I'll pay twenty remins an hour, and I'll give you free beer as long as you don't get too drunk.'

'Free beer? When do we start?' Anguson says.

'How about tonight? If you can work Fridays, Saturdays, and Sundays from ten to two, I'll give you two hundred and forty remins a week, a free drink during work hours, and one free hour with the pleasure droid of your choice. I hear you had a great time with Erica.' James winks.

'Er, no idea what you're talking about.' I look at my brown leather shoes.

'Course you do.' Anguson slaps my shoulder and laughs. 'Give Jardine two free hours with Erica and you have yourself a deal.'

'Done.' Anguson vigorously shakes James' hand.

We spend hours drinking with the men, and one or two women, disregarding the rule about getting too drunk for our shift. The conversation revolves around our hatred of San Teria, our favourite football teams, the world's greatest cage-fighters, and not one of our friends realises 'Leslie' is the former MMA world champion. The red beard and bald head are an effective disguise.

'No man alive could beat Sydney Anguson in the octagon. Just wait until he returns!' Anguson smirks.

'If you ask me, the man's over-rated – all power and no technique. Davey 'Crusher' Thompson would outclass him,' James insists and I stare at Anguson whose face has turned crimson with his nostrils flaring. Miraculously, the cage-fighter restrains the urge to reveal his true identity.

Ten o' clock arrives and Anguson and I stand on a mat between two sets of doors; the first set letting in a warm breeze. We turn away anyone who looks too drunk or rowdy, laughing off furious protests, some in the native language, but most in Anatolian. A man, with squinting eyes and spiked hair, slurs: 'I'll be back, just watch,' as he staggers away.

The foot traffic decreases so I stare at fly posters, memorising every logo and image in my boredom – a guitar player, a beer bottle, a pouting face wearing shades, a clown and a lion… My feet ache badly, but I feel fuzzy-headed so I decline James' offer to come inside the bar for a free beer. I must be losing my damn mind.

The establishment gradually fills with revellers, many younger and less ugly than the daytime customers. Anguson flirts with a trio of half-naked ladies as the man we earlier turned away stumbles along the street. He is accompanied by three friends who are walking steadily and clearly less drunk; their glares fixed on The Swine Inn.

The approaching men stare at us from head to foot; their shoulders twitching and fists clenched – one cybernetic. The drunk from earlier telegraphs a punch and Anguson ducks, pushing him onto his backside. Snorting, he pulls a flick-knife from his pocket and then two of the other men pull flick-knives, too.

One man swings his cybernetic fist and Anguson grabs his wrist, kicking straight through his knee with a crack. His upgraded hand clutches his broken leg as he squirms on the pavement.

Another man lunges at Anguson, but I punch his temple, and the cage-fighter lifts him off his feet with an uppercut. He slumps against a lamp post, blood dripping from his mouth, eyelids closed. The man who originally attacked is trembling, shoulder-to-shoulder with his one remaining friend.

'You have two choices – drop the knives and carry your friend away from here, or stay and fight – you won't live. What's it to be?' I growl.

The men exchange glances with lips quivering and they drop their flick-knives onto the lumpy stone pavement. The broken-legged cyborg sits upright and the other two men wrap his arms around their necks. They carry him along the path which is empty of revellers who crossed the road to avoid the confrontation. We collect the flick-knives and head into The Swine Inn, and I approach James Jones at the quieter side of the bar.

'You said it got a bit rowdy in here. You didn't say people might try to kill us,' I say over the chatter of the crowd.

'What do you mean? James looks over his shoulder with his eyebrows raised.

'Four guys just attacked us with knives,' I say.

'Fucking hell, what happened?' James gasps.

'Beat the crap out of two of them and they all fled, dropping their weapons,' I say.

'Shit, why don't you sit in here and have a beer? In fact, stay in for the rest of your shift,' James says.

'Good, my feet are killing me. I'm not sure I could've continued much longer,' I say.

James places two beers on the bar, then he pulls a pint for himself and sits opposite, leaving his staff to serve the queuing customers. 'Construction worker can't stay on his feet for a few hours?' James smirks as though he knows our cover story is bullshit, almost laughing in the aftermath our life and death struggle.

'It's not *that*. I have some kind of infection. I really need a doctor. I'd go to a chemist for medication, but I can't speak the language,' I say.

'I may be able to help you out. There's a medical facility I know on the other side of the river. I'll take you tomorrow and since you risked your life, I'll even pay for the treatment.'

Diagnosis

Wearing a fedora and smoking a cigarette, James leads me through a sprawling shopping mall, clearly designated for wealthy citizens, but Nusantara is not segregated like Anatolia so the poor are mixed into the crowd.

We cross a floor of turquoise tiles, passing displays of fashionable clothes and dazzling jewellery. The window of an electronics store exhibits gadgetry, including droids for entertainment and servitude, some cute and gimmicky, some human-like and highly expensive. I glance into a restaurant where a woman picks up what looks like a fried tarantula, biting it in half, and I thought Anatolia's locust fetish was weird.

Someone bumps into my injured forearm and I restrain a scream, turning to face a teenage girl with a spiral haircut, green lipstick, and angular pads poking from her shoulders. Alienesque eyes bulge in response to my tears and my whimpering. She mutters what I assume is an apology and hurries into a store.

'What is it with with these kids and their weird clothes? It feels like I'm on a different planet,' I mutter.

James and I reach an area with multiple escalators surrounding bungee trampolines for squealing kids. Heading down a level, we pass through a glass walkway and I watch pedestrians walking on a pavement below our feet. Suddenly, it seems like we are floating.

We reach an indoor market with red lighting, where stalls sell cheap clothes, dated gadgets, and 'ornamental' weapons. Every sagging face we pass is evocative of the bottom-levellers of Medio city. And the contrast with the main section of the mall could not be more pronounced.

As we navigate the crowd, flip-flops reveal dirty toenails, ragged sleeves reveal wrist stumps, and metal teeth flaunt imagined wealth and status. We enter a store stacked with phials to see a dwarf with a huge eye and a dead eye peering over the counter. 'Hello, Heather, we're here to see the doc.' The dwarf walks around the counter and opens a door which is barely noticeable due to the trinkets hanging from small hooks. We are led into a room with cybernetic parts in glass cases – titanium hands and feet, artificial eyes, and obscure items of unknown function.

'What the fuck is this place? I don't want no fucking implants. I want drugs. Just drugs,' I say.

'Relax, Leo, the doc has a stockpile of drugs and he can write prescriptions, too.' James shakes his head.

'Please take a seat and the doc will be with you shortly.'

Heather returns to the front of the store as James and I sit on a row of three seats with brown, bobbled padding. A tubular bulb on the ceiling appears to be fading; its glow barely reaching the lime walls and ruffled brown carpet. As we wait inside this cramped surgery, the hidden location and dodgy products are giving me second thoughts about treatment.

'What kind of doctor has a backroom in some dingy store?' I say.

'The affordable kind. The doc is fully qualified, but now he makes his money on narcotics, black market implants and prescriptions for immigrants. He's half the price of a decent doctor in this country, too.'

A young-ish skinny man in a white coat opens a door just a yard or two from our seats. He has a mop of black hair and a cybernetic hand which makes me nervous about the coming examination. That thing had better not malfunction when it touches my bullet wound.

'James, it's good to see you. Why don't you come on through?'

'It's not me I'm here for, Doc, it's my friend Leo. I'll be paying for his check-up.'

'Okay, Leo, come on through.' The doc points his arms into the doorway and I follow his instruction, entering a room with a wheeled bed and a desk with chairs either side. A wooden bench is covered in medical instruments and sterile packaging, and the cabinets underneath contain thin drawers. The doc and I sit at his desk which bears a compuscreen and a clipboard.

'How is it that I can help you, my friend?' the doc says.

'I have this problem with my feet, they're turning black. My hand is too, but that's probably just from being shot,' I say.

'Oh my, someone's been living a colourful life.' The doc raises his eyebrows. 'Why don't you take off your shoes and socks, and sit on the bed?'

I follow the doc's instruction and the stench of my bruised, flaking feet floods the office. The doc approaches and takes a long look, bending his legs and squinting, then he approaches my hand. 'Please roll up your sleeve.' I do as told and the doc puts a rubber glove on his human hand, then he removes the bloody dressing. The twitchy fingers of his augmentation peel the plaster and I wince as my hairs are pulled from their follicles. The bullet-hole in my forearm is near-black and the surrounding skin is bluish down to my right hand.

'Looks like necrosis. Recommended course of action – full amputation, if you can afford it. Amputation and cybernetic replacement will set you back twenty five thousand remins for your hand and feet. If you wanna skip the new hand and go for basic replacement feet, that'll be six thousand remins.'

'Are you fucking kidding me? I don't wanna cut off my hand and feet. Is there nothing you can do?'

'Well, there is a drug available. I don't have it in stock, but I can write a prescription.'

'Let me get this straight, there's a drug you can prescribe, but your first suggestion was amputation?' I say.

'Here's the thing, without treatment, your hand and feet will fall off within a few weeks. The spread of infection is only limited because your blood vessels are being destroyed. However, there's a high chance the infection could spread through your body, particularly if you get another open wound. If it does, you're dead.'

'Fuck. So what about this drug?' I say.

'Fifty-fifty chance of partial recovery, but you'll probably never regain full motorfunction in these parts. If you don't show signs of recovery within ten days, or if there is any indication of further spread, amputation will be the only option.'

I sit upright with my legs hanging over the bed, puffing my cheeks as I stare at my rotting bullet wound, unsure if I am being scammed. The doc stands back and folds his arms, nodding sympathetically.

'Just give me the prescription, please. No offence, but I hope to the Goddess I never see you again.'

The doc cleans my wound with an antiseptic wipe, bandages my forearm, then cleans his metal hand with fluid. I put on my socks and shoes as the doc writes a prescription, saying: 'I couldn't stitch the wound due to the surrounding damage, but your medication should aid the healing process. Take one pill a day and do not mix with alcohol. These tablets are very strong.'

I return to James who pays twenty remins for my consultation, and the doc says: 'Have a think about those cybernetics,' as we leave his surgery.

My walk becomes a painful hobble as we travel to a pharmacy a few streets away from the mall. After a short wait staring at medical supplies, I collect my prescription, tear open the tiny box, and pop a pill out of the packaging. I swallow without water, then ignore the doc's advice to take one pill a day, swallowing two more. I am not losing my hand and feet to necrosis.

'So what's the story?' James asks as we descend the river bank towards the swing-bridge.

'Story?'

'Your feet don't turn black for nothing. And your hand... If the doc suggested cybernetic replacement, it must be bad.'

'You wanna know the tr-truth?' I pause in a spell of dizziness, probably due to my pills. My head clears after a few deep breaths and I fix James' gaze. 'Bullet in the arm, and a bad case of trench foot.'

'You're ex-military, aren't you? I knew it,' James says.

'Didn't wanna say at first, but being in The Swine Inn, it's clear I'm among friends.' I correct my footing, almost hobbling into a lamp post. 'They wanted me to continue fighting; just bandaged me up and said get on with it. Didn't even give me fucking stitches. Now it's too late for them. My arm's a mess. Better hope these pills clear up the infection before too much of my flesh rots. Doc reckons I've got ten days to avoid am... amp... er, amputation.'

'Leo, are you okay-ay?'

'Yeah... I'm fine...' I scratch my head as a group of indistinct figures pass by with their faces blurring, hair streaking upwards like candle flames. My eyes refocus and I glance to James whose grey skin momentarily shimmers.

'That's pretty rough-gh...' James says; his voice fading as though he is distant. *'You're certainly among friends... more so than you realise... all the men are in the same boat... take care of our own... need a few days off to recover... just let me know, soldier-dier...'*

My thigh muscles burn as we cross the swing-bridge which tilts sideways and I seek the railing with my heart pounding. The entire structure wobbles and I fall into the arms of James who somehow maintains his footing during this violent tremor. My head flops back and the clouds swirl in a vortex like a tornado is brewing.

'Are you sure you're okay-ay?'

'Y-yeah, I, er, I dunno...'

'Maybe you're reacting to the medication-ation.'

'Probably because I tripled the d-dosage.'

'Well, that was a dumb idea-ea.'

My thigh muscles cool as the clouds settle and the swing-bridge corrects its position before we plunge into the river. I take a few breaths, then break from James' grasp and we plod towards the other bank. The climb is exhausting, but we soon reach The Swine Inn and I find Anguson in the entertainment room, playing poker with July on his knee.

A number of men are sitting at the table which is covered in playing cards, remin notes, and spilt beer. A pleasure droid is standing behind a man in a flat cap, rubbing his shoulder; the other droids are sitting at a table in the corner, pouting as cigarette smoke swirls.

'The fuck you doing, wasting our money?' I sneer.

'What, a man can't relax with his friends?' Anguson's grin stretches wide and his teeth sharpen into points. *'I'll raise you twenty-ty-ty...'*

The occupants of the table move in slow-motion; their features smudging and distorting in the darkness as laughter echoes. A terrible pain afflicts my right arm which bulges and tears through my sleeve: black, scaly, slithering. I reel as a trio of snakeheads replace my fingers and one hisses and lunges for my nose, just missing. A voice asks: *'Are you okay-ay?'* as the snakes transform into a hand of rotting flesh.

Shaking my head, I leave the entertainment room and clutch the bannister as I venture upstairs to recuperate. The bedroom spins as I lie down – dresser, mirror, lampshade, wardrobe, all swirling around the rocking bed. I switch between phases of dizziness and calmness with each episode decreasing in severity; the spinning slower and shorter in duration, but still enough to stop me from sleeping.

Hours pass and I go one long hour without an episode so I return downstairs and sit with Asias at the front bar. The doc's instruction not to mix drugs and alcohol is reluctantly followed to avoid further side-effects. I order a pint of water from James which I gulp down, ordering another and sitting in silence. The big screen is showing war footage in the background, and Asias is leaning on his elbows with his eyes low.

'Just heard on the news, Anatolian warships are two hundred miles from the coast. We can expect invasion any day now. A bunch of the men have signed up to the Nusantaran military. I can understand why. Part of me is tempted to join them,' Asias says.

'And risk ending up in a box? Your boy needs to meet his father again.' I wipe my sweaty brow.

'And he needs to know I'm not a failure, a coward, a deserter. If Anatolia win this war, what will his future be? Poverty? Tyranny? He deserves so much better.' Asias' eyes fill with water but fail to form tears. 'My boy's special and not just in an every-dad-thinks-his-kid-is-special kind'a way. That's why I named him Arturo – it means strong as a bear. He'll go onto great things, but only if I provide the opportunity.'

As I clutch my glass, I drop my head and sigh through pursed lips. 'In all this shit, I've been so concerned about my future, I almost forgot it's not just about us... I guess that's what fatherhood does, reminds you there's something greater than yourself. When you speak of your son, I believe what you say, and you're right that San Teria need to be stopped.'

'And that won't happen unless good men like us unite against them.'

'Maybe you and I will join the fight, or maybe we'll have to accept we're not cut out for this shit. You're exhibiting signs of PTSD. You could be a liability on the battlefield, and so could I with my injuries.'

'You mean your hand? I noticed it's in bad shape.' Asias nods to my swollen navy hand.

'That's what a bullet does to you, puts you in bad shape. And then there's the fucking trench foot.'

'I really shouldn't be surprised to discover you're ex-military. You and Leslie – one glance should have been enough to see you were more than just construction workers.'

BACK TO WHAT WE DO BEST

'SO HOW COME YOU WEREN'T WORKING the door last night?' Anguson sits on my bed without July as I shield my eyes from sunlight burning through the leaf-print curtains. I must have left the bedroom door unlocked in my delirium, but at least the snake fingers are gone.

'Medical reasons. The doc gave me some pills; knocked the stuffing out of me. I needed to rest,' I say.

'And you complained about *me* wasting money? You lazy bastard,' Anguson says.

'I wasn't the one gambling.' I sit up in bed, fully-clothed with a fuzzy head and dry mouth. My sweaty shirt sticks to my chest as I stretch my arms. 'How much did you lose, anyways?'

'Not much, a couple of hundred remins–'

'A couple of hundred remins? Have you lost your damn mind?' I grab my medication and swallow a pill, leaving the packet on the dresser.

'Relax, it's not like there's a rush to get home. I'm having fun here. Earning enough to scrape by. Surrounded by good men, a beautiful woman...' Anguson says.

'You're surrounded by a bunch of drunken savages and a rubber doll. And you just blew a week's wages in one night,' I say, suddenly not so keen to stick around, now that my hand could be forced by Anguson's stupidity.

'We can earn that back in one robbery... How about today? I'm thinking gambling shop. Got the idea during the card game,' Anguson says.

'How do we find a gambling shop in this place? We can't read a single door sign. And then there's the small problem of giving instructions to a clerk who doesn't speak Anatolian. How the hell will they understand us?' I say.

'They'll understand this KAL Ten. Come on, every gambling shop in the world looks the same. Just grab that pillow case,' Anguson says.

'What, why?' I frown, glancing at my drool-covered, flowery pillow case.

'For the money, genius.'

I climb out of bed, remove my sticky shirt, strap on my holster, and stuff the pillow case inside a fresh shirt. Skipping a much-needed shower, I follow my accomplice into the streets to seek out a gambling shop. The sun is blazing so we purchase two bottles of fizzy pop from a newsagent, gulping them down and belching. We stare into windows whenever we spot signs displaying Nusantaran numbers on the assumption they are betting odds.

A pair of greasy foreigners attract stares as we identify our mark, squinting through window glare and whispering. We march into the gambling shop which has two screens before each till, separated by horizontal arm-width gaps. To make things more convenient, one of the screens is missing and a pretty young lady is sitting behind the gap.

Anguson aims his machine pistol at her teary face and she raises her hands, trembling. I pull the pillow case from my shirt and hand it to the crying girl, then I aim my machine pistol at the staff members, one by one. Each empties the contents of their tills into the pillow case which is now stuffed with cash.

A chubby man bursts through a door and his shirt instantly fills with bullet holes, turning from peach to red with a deafening roar. He drops his shotgun, falls to his knees and thuds onto his face, courtesy of Anguson's machine pistol. Poor bastard.

The staff are cowering, screaming as blood streams over tiles and Anguson leans over the counter. 'Hand over the fucking money!' The woman controls her trembling hand to obey and my accomplice snatches the pillow case as the corpse twitches. We flee the premises, running between braking cars, down several alleys and stopping for breath.

'What now? It's gonna be pretty difficult making it through town without raising suspicion.' I slot my weapon into my holster and button my shirt with screams still ringing in my ears.

'Why didn't you suggest a getaway vehicle, Jardine? Would'a made things so much easier.'

'Oh, so this is *my* fault now? This is the last time we do an armed robbery. It's too risky and that bloke shouldn't have died to help our shitty situation,' I say.

'Stupid bastard would be alive now if he didn't act the hero.'

We march through Batavia with a pillow case full of notes, and every passing civilian stares at our sweaty mugs, tempting me to withdraw my weapon. My gaze constantly shifts to check for police, but they do not emerge and we safely reach The Swine Inn.

We hurry upstairs without greeting the bar staff or regulars and we enter Anguson's bedroom. July is sitting before the dresser mirror with her skinny legs crossed. She stops humming to whisper, 'Hello'. My accomplice locks the door and I approach the bay window, still watching for cops in my ultra-paranoid state, then I draw the curtains. Anguson empties the pillow case, covering the ruffled quilt in remin notes, and we add the cash from our pockets to the pile.

'July, do me a favour, count the money, please,' Anguson says.

The pleasure droid snatches the notes at blurring speed, putting them into neat piles on the dresser. 'That's eighteen thousand, three hundred and thirty remins.' July turns with a smile and places her hands behind her backside. I cram half the notes into my pockets so Anguson cannot squander our funds.

'Enough to get us home,' I say and a warmth spreads over my cheeks, subduing my shame.

'But do we really wanna go, just now?' Anguson lowers his head, fixing my gaze.

'What?'

'Let's face it, Anatolia's a shit-hole. I mean this place is too, but I'm starting to feel like I belong,' Anguson says.

'Let's take July to the airport.' I say sternly. 'She can buy the tickets. Then we'll take her back to James as a going away present, if we have time.'

'I can't give away the love of my life!' Anguson laughs loudly and coarsely, then glances to July with saddened eyes and pouts his bottom lip.

'Have lost your damn mind? You've plenty to go back to, unlike most,' I say.

'Conscription you mean? My money's as good as useless at home or abroad.'

'Neither of us are getting conscripted. We'll go into hiding until this war is over. Anatolia's a big place,' I say.

Anguson and I remove our holsters, weapons, and ammunition to avoid alerting airport security, and we leave The Swine Inn. We hail a taxi with a solar cell exterior and July instructs the driver to head to the airport. My knees tremble during the journey, but the rearview mirror shows Anguson smiling as July strokes his red beard.

On the outskirts of Batavia, I spot a huge, concave roof supported by slanted beams and walls of tinted glass. A scramjet ascends to the clouds, confirming we have reached our destination, but as the taxi driver parks, the presence of armed cops is disconcerting. I pay the fare and we exit the vehicle, marching tensely towards one of the guarded entrances. The assault rifles on display are not only unnecessary, but more dangerous than phasers in a civilian-packed area. These officers want to intimidate and they are succeeding.

A cop points his rifle and tilts his head – his eyes, nostrils, and gaping mouth are strangely dark – like scorch marks on leathery skin. I make eye contact for a fraction of a second, switching my gaze to straight ahead to avoid provocation. We rigidly enter a revolving door, but the armed cops in the crowd mean we cannot relax just yet.

'July, can you take us to a ticket kiosk?' I ask and the pleasure droid leads over a brown floor of square and round tiles. We pass a long pot containing five mini-trees, coming to one of several self-service booths – a wavy column of metal with a screen, keypad, and two slots for credit cards and remin notes. I remove some money from my pocket. 'July, you'll need to book two tickets on the next flight to Scania, and from there two tickets to Anatolia. Any city will do, just get us home.'

July taps the touchscreen to browse ticket menus and she says: 'There is a flight to Gamla Stan airport, Scania, on fourteenth September at ten past midnight.'

'Perfect, book the tickets, please,' I say.

'Each ticket is eight hundred and eighty remins,' July says.

I hand over about two thousand remins and July taps the touchscreen, then slots the notes into the machine. Our change drops into a half-bowl as the tickets are printed, and the pleasure droid places them into my hands.

'Right, we need tickets from Gamla Stan airport to anywhere in Anatolia on fourteenth September or after.' I put the coins into my trouser pocket.

'There are tickets available from Gamla Stan airport to Gaeliao airport on seventeenth September at seven-thirty p.m.'

'Three days apart, fuck it, I'll sleep on the airport floor if I have to.' I give more money to July. 'Purchase the tickets, please.'

July purchases the plane tickets and I collect them from her grasp, jumping as a male voice yells in Nusantaran. The chatter of the airport goes silent as three cops charge through the parting crowd with assault rifles readied. They surround a man near an escalator and I breathe a sigh of relief as his hands are cuffed.

We leave the airport to queue for a taxi and I shuffle the plane tickets, staring as though to check they are real. I could swear the paper is glistening like gold, and I refuse to let the tickets out of my grasp, even to put them in my pocket.

'We're actually going home,' I mutter; my voice almost breaking into laughter.

'Just out of curiosity, July, what is today's date?' Anguson says as the pleasure droid clutches his forearm.

'Today is twenty-fifth of August, twenty-thirty.'

'You seriously mean to tell me we've got three more weeks till departure?' I say.

'No, twenty days,' July says.

'Oh, that makes it much better. Fucking great,' I say.

CELEBRATION

WE TAKE A TAXI BACK TO THE SWINE INN and head upstairs as Anguson sings terribly about how *'we're going home'*. So much for wanting to stay in Batavia. A hot flush and dizzy spell make me grab the banister as the thinly-carpeted staircase creaks. I reach the third floor where the paintings of ships in stormy seas momentarily come to life.

Upon entering my bedroom, I lock the door and put the tickets into a drawer, along with the money and guns, underneath my clothes. We have lots of change from our robberies which only intensifies the guilt and shame about the loss of human life, but we are, and always have been, bastards. Bottom-levellers do what it takes to survive.

I attempt to clench the aching fingers of my right hand, but they barely move. The veins are bright blue and the skin is navy with flecks of black, flaking. The itching is relentless and I have no idea whether the pills are preventing cell decay, let alone reversing it.

Anguson is gazing into July's eyes as she sits on his knee; her artificial cleavage perpetuating the illusion of infatuation, and his groping hands could not care less. Her lips are yellow today, her hair and eyelids yellow, pink and turquoise, her vest and shorts black and gold. This pleasure droid is a fucking chameleon.

I lie across the soft bed with arms spread, resting my eyelids, but Anguson immediately interrupts: 'Come on, let's celebrate. We've got money to burn. Let's have a few beers, play some cards, maybe you can request the company of Erica.'

I roll my eyes and sit up slowly, but if I cannot celebrate on a day like today, when can I celebrate? We head downstairs to the entertainment room and the pleasure droids are sitting at the corner table, giggling like they enjoy one another's company. *Creepy*. Erica waves, but I avert my gaze to order a beer for Anguson and a shandy for myself.

Three men are playing cards at a table; each of them dishevelled, clad in black and brown, overdressed for the heat, but ready for the nuclear winter this world is heading towards.

'Steve, Taiwo, and, er–'

'Johnson,' a man with fat lips and stubble says.

'Mind if we join the next game?' Anguson says.

'Take a seat,' Johnson says and we pull chairs to the table as the round of poker ends. Taiwo shuffles the cards, dealing Anguson and me into the game; his 'wife' is just here to watch. As I peek at my cards, Johnson glances at my right hand; the corner of his mouth curling downwards in disgust.

'Looks bad. If I was you, I'd be raising the funds for cybernetic replacement. It isn't so prone to human frailty. If you ask me, it's better in every way.' Johnson raises his metallic hand, and like so many cyborgs, he has not acquired artificial skin. Strange fashion statement.

'Any problems with co-ordination?' I ask as the men take turns raising the stakes.

'Only once. I suspect it was electromagnetic interference or some shit. My fingers wouldn't stop wriggling for twenty minutes. Other than that, I haven't had a problem,' Johnson says.

'But you see, that's my problem. It's not really *your* hand, so you're not fully in control. I don't want to become a malfunctioning robot. No offence,' I say.

'Looks like you're not functioning too great, right now,' Johnson says.

'Well, I can't argue with that. The way I'm going, maybe I'll have no choice in the matter.' I glance to the card dealer. 'Er, I fold.'

The men slide their cards into the middle of the table and Johnson collects the pile to take his turn to deal. He shuffles quickly with multiple techniques, showing an impressive degree of control over the cards.

'Now I can understand how a cybernetic hand is more capable than a human one, but I can't understand how the brain is capable of increased motorcontrol. Is it you, or is there some microchip, or some shit, doing the extra computation?' I say.

'Ya know, I've never thought about that. I just know this hand is better than my old one. And then there's my artificial eyes.' Johnson places the deck down. 'Check this out. Ya see the empty bottle on that table? Go over to it.' I leave my seat to approach the bottle five yards away, and Johnson continues: 'Now hold it up. I bet you I can read the label from here.' I hold up the empty beer bottle. 'Brown Ale is affectionately known as Dog to the people who drink it. This is because *I'm going to see a man about a dog* was often used as an excuse by men to sneak off to the pub for a pint... Need I go on?'

'That's pretty impressive. The letters are so small I can barely read them from here,' I say.

Placing the bottle down, I return to my seat to play poker, and alcohol seems to be reacting with my tablets because I suddenly feel lousy. My head hurts, in fact my eyeballs hurt, and yet I sip shandies until my speech is slurring; the voice in my head whispering *just one more* each time I finish.

After about two hours, our poker game ends with Johnson winning a large pile of remins.

'Hey James, how about getting Tara to strip for us?' Taiwo booms over the rhythm and blues music, and the men yell: 'Yeah', raising their glasses to the scantily-clad pleasure droids in the corner.

James Jones lifts the hinged section of the bar and approaches our table with a plastic cup, saying: 'You know the drill, five remins from each of you.' The men fill the cup with remin notes and James stares at me, raising his eyebrows.

'But I don't ev…' The men fix my gaze with frowns. 'Ah, never mind.' I put five remins into the cup to contribute towards a performance I have no interest in watching.

James visits the other tables to collect money and then he approaches Tara, issuing the instruction to strip. The men cheer as she, *it*, walks onto the dance-floor and sways to the music, gradually peeling off her clothes to reveal her athletic, brown body. She approaches tables, thrusting her rubber pussy into grinning faces, and eager hands grope her arse which has been violated by half the men in here.

'She almost makes me wish I had two dicks.' Steve drools as Tara approaches our table; her big titties bouncing with every step.

'What the fuck would you do with two dicks?' I shake my head.

'I dunno, er–'

'I prefer the real thing,' Asias interrupts, joining our table with pint glass in hand.

'You don't know what you're missing out on, mate. Half an hour in a room with Tara and you'd change your tune,' Steve says.

'Nah, I've got the real thing back home. Ortellia's worth the wait,' Asias says.

'I hate to break this to you, but you could be waiting months or even years. Ya know it's not really cheating if it's a robot,' Steve says.

'The money you men spend on these things, you're gonna be flat broke. You do realise work'll be scarce if war breaks out here? If I were you, I'd be saving,' Asias says.

'Says he who spends every second at the bar.' Steve stares into his pint and gulps the froth in the bottom.

'Hey, there's no work this week and I need something to take my mind off this shit,' Asias says.

'*Exactly*.'

Anguson rises from his seat and selects hip-hop music on the jukebox, invoking memories of our childhood days in the noughties. As the speakers boom, the entertainment room fills with drunken dancers 'singing' to lyrics about 'bitches' and 'drugs' and 'guns'. Charming.

I am certainly not one for dancing, but after *just one more* shandy, I find myself joining in the fun and games. As I sway and stumble, Erica's face appears before my blurry eyes – grinning, pouting, gurning – and I lack the strength to push her away. A bout of dizziness becomes intense as my legs weaken and I fall to the sticky dancefloor…

PROPOSITION

I WAKE IN MY BED with yet another stinking hangover, looking to my side to see no pleasure droid this time. Thank fuck. Hours pass as I lie in the faint yellow glow of the curtains, motionless, close to vomiting, too exhausted to get up.

My hand and feet are itching worse than ever, like scabs ready to fall off, and no amount of scratching relieves my discomfort. I swallow another pill, tempted to visit the doc and see about those cybernetic replacements, after all. I would not have to raise too much cash and what are a few innocent bystanders if it ends *my* suffering? I cannot believe I just considered that. Fucking scumbag.

I hobble to the sink, wincing with every step, and I take large gulps of water, soaking my shirt in the process. I grab a towel and clean clothes, leave my bedroom, and cross the landing to the shower. Stripping naked, I see the darkness of my hand and feet is spreading across my arm and legs. This does not look good.

I switch on the shower, emptying my testicles under a hot spray and ignoring a knock on the door. My fluids vanish down the plughole and I sit on rough plastic, peeling off my soaking bandage. The bullet-hole in my forearm is gooey and black, like oil, and I prod the edge but feel nothing. The tissue around the wound is completely dead and the rest of my forearm severely bruised.

We have close to fourteen grand left and another successful robbery could raise the additional eleven grand for surgery, but I cannot just cut off my own flesh, can I?

I dry my putrid body, put on clean clothes, grab my dirty laundry and bandage, and leave the bathroom. July barges past me, giggling as Anguson smacks her arse and follows her inside, slamming the door. And I am not sure taking an electronic device into a shower is a good idea.

Back in my bedroom, I take a bandage from the First Aid kit, dress my gooey forearm, and bin the used bandage. I take my laundry to a washroom downstairs, paying five remins for the service, then I join James at the bar, nursing my hangover with a shandy. I have a serious problem.

'Leslie and I are gonna be leaving in three weeks. Booked our tickets yesterday.' I take a tiny sip of shandy, thinking I should have maybe ordered water.

'Returning to Anatolia?' James says.

'That's the plan. We've got to detour through Scania due to the lack of direct flights,' I say.

'I'll be sorry to see you go. You've been good customers. You're not planning on doing anything crazy like rejoining the military, are you?' James says.

'Fuck no, I'd fight *against* San Teria if it came down to it,' I say.

'I thought as much.' James wipes the bar with a cloth. 'What if I told you, you *could* help the fight against San Teria?'

'How do you mean?' I squint one eye, pausing.

'You're not the only one returning home. Many ex-military are making their way back. As you know, some have been talking to the Nusantarans and Nyberuns, signing up to their armies, but some have other plans.'

'Other plans?' I fix James' gaze.

'Between you and me, there are plans to build an insurgency group back home. The aim is to bring down the government and put an end to this damn war.'

'That's a bold ambition, but what help could we be?' I say.

'Are you kidding? You're ex-military, tough. You seem smart, too. This insurrection shouldn't involve direct fighting. We'd be talking espionage, the destruction of infrastructure, the recruitment of others – make the movement as big as possible, turn the tide against San Teria.'

'Whoa, that's a hell of a lot to think about.' I gulp my beer, lean back and stare at the golden pattern in the carpet.

'You don't have to decide right away, but think of this – we'll be able to help you hide. You're gonna need to lie low. Remember, the penalty for desertion is death.'

A customer approaches the bar in high heels so I turn on my stool to watch Johnson playing pool in the corner. The short and stocky ex-soldier clears the table with ease, pulling off trick-shots thanks to his cybernetic hand. His opponent curls his lips and watches helplessly, not getting one shot. 'That'll be twenty remins, please.' Johnson holds out his human palm as the black ball sinks into the pocket.

'Fuck that, I'm not giving you twenty remins,' his beaten opponent says.

'We had a bet. I won fair and square.' Johnson growls.

'You didn't tell me your metal hand would give you special skills.'

'It's not like I was hiding it. My hand was in full view and you offered the bet... I suggest you pay.' Johnson clenches his teeth and the cue in his cybernetic hand breaks into splintered halves, falling to the floor. The surrounding men step back, gawping as James leaves the bar and approaches the confrontation, glaring.

'Right, I want your winnings to pay for a new cue. One of you can give me twenty remins or both of you are leaving.'

The loser pouts and hands over twenty remins to the furious landlord without further protest. James mutters under his breath as he returns to the bar and places the money in his till drawer. Asias orders a beer and as he picks up his pint, I notice the letters A.S.T.R. tattooed on his forearm.

'What does that stand for?' I say and Asias hesitates, crumpling his brow so I nod to the elaborate green lettering.

'Oh, the tattoo? It stands for Alliance of San Terian Renegades. It's our *Fuck You* to the Elites for the oath we were forced to swear. Our way of saying you don't own us... Of course, it makes return a bit riskier, given that we have identifying marks,' Asias whispers.

'But those identifying marks help you feel part of a cause?' I say.

'I know, pathetic, isn't it? Posing as part of an imaginary army when I have PTSD, but I need to do something. I can't just sit this one out. I won't have my boy grow up thinking his Daddy's a coward.'

'I wouldn't say pathetic – it shows commitment. Returning to Anatolia was always gonna be dangerous, but you could be an asset to the Rebellion. Go home, rejoin your family and make a difference,' I say.

'I've been thinking about it, but I'd need to sort out a Citicard first,' Asias says.

'Fuck, I didn't even think about that. Bought plane tickets yesterday and thought they'd just let us on the plane. What a fucking idiot...'

'That's what stress does to ya.' Asias nods sympathetically but just makes me feel stupider. 'I know of a man who sells the Citicards of dead ex-pats for fifteen hundred remins. I can't afford one, right now, but I can take you and Leslie. Only problem is, the guy doesn't speak Anatolian.'

'That's fine, July is fluent in one hundred and seventy nine languages,' I say.

'Well, we may as well go now if you've got nothing better to do,' Asias says.

Asias and I finish our drinks and head to the third floor of the inn, and I knock on the varnished panel of Anguson's bedroom door. The shirtless oaf opens up to reveal July standing naked, plugged into a wall socket via a cable joined to her ankle. Asias stares at her bare arse and curved hips with his tongue hanging out.

'Citicards,' I say.

'What?' Anguson scratches his head and stares with puffy eyes.

'What kind of idiots think they can take a flight without Citicards?' I say.

'Oh, fucking hell!' Anguson booms.

'Get ya clothes on. We're going to see a guy, but we'll need July to speak the language,' I say.

Once the lovebirds are dressed, the four of us head across the river, coming to market stalls with animals in cages – local delicacies like chickens, dogs, and cats. We walk below canopies which allow sunlight through slender gaps, shining on the fruit and vegetables.

We come to a large doorway aligned with glowing green windows bearing black symbols. As we venture inside the building, wavy mirrors distort our reflections, and strange plants grow from ornamental pots – tall stems with red leaves like blood droplets. We pass through the crowded tables to a bar and as we queue, Asias says: 'July, you'll need to tell them we're here to meet Hosu.'

July relays the instruction to a barmaid who raises a finger, then leaves the bar and disappears around a corner. She emerges a minute or so later, and leads us through a door with two guards into a private room. A bald man with piercings in his face is sitting on a throne with curved iron spikes – presumably this is Hosu. Or the Emperor of Nusantara, perhaps.

A wolf with green-tinged fur is sleeping in the corner, goons are glaring from the tables, and paintings of trees and mountains cover the walls. The man on the throne talks gibberish in a deep voice and Asias says: 'July, explain to him that we're Anatolian and that Leslie and Leo require Citicards.'

July relays the instruction and then she relays the man's reply: 'He says they'll need to replace your fingerprints so they match the biometric data on the Citicards. The cost will be three thousand, six hundred remins.'

'Fuck, that's more than anticipated... Fine,' I say.

The man on a throne waves to a goon wearing a grey hat and he mutters gibberish in his deep voice. The goon leaves through a door in the corner and returns minutes later, holding a small white device. He reaches for my right hand, hesitating as he spots the discolouration of my skin. I offer my left hand and he places my index finger into the device which clamps shut.

My fingertip burns as the skin cells are restructured and I restrain my trembling until the process is complete. The man rewrites all five fingerprints on my left hand and then my numbed right hand, grimacing at the discolouration. He does the same to Anguson and then says something and waves his hand outwards.

'Go and wait in the bar. He'll find you when he's ready. Make sure you have the money,' July says.

We head to a decked area outside with orange lanterns hanging above table umbrellas. A pair of snarling men are arm-wrestling in a crowded corner, causing Anguson's eyes to light up. Asias brings us beers and I am wary about them reacting with my medication, but the shandies have not yet caused an issue. Well, apart from when I collapsed yesterday. Anyways, I do not feel groggy so fuck it, I am drinking that beer.

An hour or so passes, and three beers later, the barmaid returns and leads us into the room where the goon in a grey hat is holding brown packages.

We hand over the money and he mutters gibberish with a frown as we collect our Citicards.

'He says do not open them on or near the premises,' July says, and we return to the decking area with our packages to drink *one more beer*.

As I sip my pint, I am overcome by dizziness so I rest my face on my forearm and breathe heavily. Anguson wanders across the decking as Asias says something like: 'Cheer you up,' in an echoey voice and places something into my hand. I stare at two tiny, fuzzy, yellow things, and watch Asias put two of them into his mouth. I do the same with a shrug and gulp down the rest of my beer.

Asias speaks with a wide grin, but I do not understand a word and just nod as he jabbers away. My heart pounds as I feel intense anxiety and I can sense Asias is mocking me in some foreign language... I strongly suspect he is planning to attack and steal my money, the treacherous bastard... What am I going to do?

As I consider running away, I stroke my cheekbones in horror because my skin is melting, dripping onto the table. My face forms a gooey puddle as I touch my bare skull, teeth, eye sockets. *He* must have did this... I... I...

Everything goes black... *Next thing, Anguson is roaring as he slams a hand onto a table, collects remin notes from his beaten opponent, and takes the hand of the next arm-wrestler.*

Everything goes black... *Next thing, snarling men lunge at Anguson, only to get lifted off their feet by uppercuts. Anguson takes July by the hand and dances to piano music as the crowd clear the deck.*

Everything goes black... *Next thing, I am dancing with a girl too ugly to be a pleasure droid in a room with pink flowers on the walls. Asias laughs and says, 'Looks like he's cheered up now' as he pats my back.*

Everything goes black... *Next thing, I am watching praying mantises fight among a crowd of roaring men. One slices through the other's wing with its pincer and then decapitates its wounded foe.*

Everything goes black... *Next thing, I am sitting beside a swimming pool with bikini-clad girls around me, and I smack a jiggling arse, only to receive a glare.*

Everything goes black... *Next thing, I am sitting in a temple, soaking wet and surrounded by red lion-head statues as worshippers chant.*

And so the transitioning continues, and I am not sure what is real or imaginary until I end up at a familiar place – The Swine Inn.

THE FORMATION OF THE REBELLION

I AM AWOKEN BY A BOOMING KNOCK at the door, only to discover my bedroom is filled with pink balloons and golden glitter. What the fuck? I button up my shirt, squinting due to the glaring sunlight, and I wade through the balloons to unlock the door. Anguson and July barge into my bedroom, and the pleasure droid hands over a mysterious brown package, muttering: 'You lost something?'

Reaching out slowly, I collect the package from July's grasp, then I reply: 'Oh fuck, the Citicard!' I tear open the paper and remove a small bottle with the words: *for the eye scanner* scrawled on the front – must be the contact lenses so I place the bottle in my pocket.

The last object in the packaging is a green plastic rectangle with an embedded microchip. I hold the Citicard to the window light and read my new personal details:

Name: Charles Brewster
DOB: 7/3/88
Birth Place: Etoxeti

'No way I'll pass for forty-two... Will I?' I mutter under my breath.

'Eh?' Anguson says as I scratch behind my ear and then he mumbles something, squeezing the arse of the pleasure droid.

'Uh, what?' I say.

'You were off your nut last night. Looked like you were having a great time, though.' Anguson laughs.

'Let's go downstairs,' I say as July plays with the pink balloons, rolling on the glittery carpet and giggling. I put the Citicard and contact lens bottle into the drawer with my gun and clothes, and we leave the bedroom. The three of us sit on stools at the bar and I stare at a white circular clock hanging over a doorway – it is 12:30pm.

'I don't even wanna know what the glitter on your face is all about,' James says as I purchase a pint of water, then rub my cheeks.

My change slips through my fingers as booming thunder causes the glasses to shake, and the patrons exchange glances. Lightning flashes and splashes leap from my glass as thunder booms again, followed by a gentle but ominous rattling. Another booming is even louder, ear-splitting, and my glass hits my teeth as I sip cold water. This is no natural phenomenon.

The patrons gossip in confusion as July strokes Anguson's greasy face, then Steve runs into the bar, yelling: 'Anatolian troops have reached Batavia; some of them were taking pot-shots at civilians. I saw a little girl gunned down for no reason. When I was coming back, rockets were fired at buildings. One collapsed before my eyes. The invasion has begun!'

'Our own people gunning down civilians? I've seen collateral damage on active duty, but murder?' I say.

'Nusantarans have been portrayed as subhuman for a long time and now they're colluding with the enemy. It wouldn't take much to persuade the bloodthirsty among the ranks to commit mass slaughter,' James says.

'They'll be aiming to create terror and anarchy.' Taiwo approaches the bar. 'I'm guessing their next targets will be infrastructure – the power grid, water supply – break the will of the people.'

'One thing's for sure, no-one is safe. If you own a gun, best arm yourself. We may need to fight, but my advice right now is do not leave these premises. If you try to flee, they could be waiting.' Steve withdraws a handgun from his jacket and a few others do the same.

'Let's get the fucking guns,' Anguson says, and every guest at the inn, including us, rushes upstairs to our rooms.

Anguson and I strap our holsters on the outside of our shirts, then I look out the bay window, but see nothing out of the ordinary as I close the curtains. We return downstairs with KAL 10's on display. Almost everyone in the bar is wielding some kind of firearm, and some of the men are whispering about joining the fight once the Nusantaran military arrive.

Keys jangle as James locks the front doors and puts the local news on the big screen. Although I cannot understand a word, the footage of rocket attacks says all I need to know: Blinding white flashes. A cityscape filling with smoke. The local population falling by the second.

'That looks like a fucking school,' Steve mutters as a large building is reduced to rubble, and a tear rolls down his cheek.

'We have to stop these bastards,' James growls, then he stands before the big screen and clears his throat. 'It's time for serious talk about this insurrection we've got planned. There's no point in secrecy anymore. I think most, if not all of us, have a deep-rooted hatred of San Teria. Although their military is composed of our people, they're fighting for the enemy so they must be treated accordingly. Is everyone in agreement, the invaders are now our enemy?'

'Aye!' the men roar.

'We have two options. Either we join the Nusantaran military or we return to Anatolia and commence the insurrection movement,' James says.

The men gossip among themselves, some talking about returning home, some saying they want to fight directly, others expressing reservations about killing men who could be their own friends.

'What about this insurrection movement?' Anguson says, having not been present during our previous conversation.

'The plan is to bring down the government.' James approaches our stools, staring intensely. 'Our numbers are small, but I doubt recruitment is gonna be a problem. If you join us, your main task will likely be taking down Anatolian infrastructure. Ya know, planting bombs and shit.'

'Might be a little problematic for me to get involved, given how recognisable I am,' Anguson says.

'What the fuck are you talking about?' James says in a raised voice.

'Okay, I'm not so recognisable. The red beard has clearly thrown you.' Anguson gulps his beer and fixes James' gaze. 'I am more than just a Sydney Anguson lookalike.'

James crumples his brow, laughs, and says: 'Fuck off!' as he slaps the bar with both hands. Thunder booms and lamp-shades swing as the patrons hunch, knowing the next target could be The Swine Inn. I compose myself as the booming subsides and say: 'True story. I served with the bastard from the day he joined.'

The men gather at the bar, staring at the celebrity in their midst, tugging at his red beard. A woman pushes through the crowd and squeezes Anguson's biceps, then places her fingers over her lips, blushing.

'How the hell didn't I see this before? Six foot seven, built like a brick shithouse. I feel like an idiot,' Asias says and everyone laughs as though they share the sentiment.

'Don't we all?' James shakes his head as the laughter calms; his eyes glazed. 'So we've got the world's greatest cage-fighter in our ranks…'

'I seem to remember you insisting Davey 'Crusher' Thompson was better than me, just the other night.'

'Er, well, I was a little drunk.' James looks down, sheepishly. 'Anyways, a high-profile figure would be perfect for us. You could record videos speaking out against San Teria, undermine their authority, challenge the propaganda, turn the tide of public opinion.'

'And get quartered for my troubles.' Anguson sighs.

'You'd need to keep hidden, either way. You're a deserter. Look, I've got contacts in Underworld, among other places. Nothing but crooks down there. You could lie low, help us run things behind the scenes, become a figurehead. Not every man needs to be on the front line.' James takes a stool and rests on the bar.

'Well, I tell you what, I really do hate those San Terian bastards, but I wouldn't be keen on killing my army friends. This could be a perfect compromise,' Anguson says.

'This is good to hear. Let's just hope we can get you on that plane. It's very possible flights will be grounded. I can't wait to see the look on Hitchens' face when I tell him Sydney Anguson has joined our ranks,' James says.

'Hitchens?' Anguson says.

'One of the Rebellion's commanders, if commander is the right word. We're hardly an army right now, but that's what we plan to become,' James says.

'That's interesting, James. We'll continue this conversation in a minute. Excuse me while I take a piss.' Anguson rises from his stool and the others watch him head to the men's room as though they are still processing his true identity – I remember the feeling.

'So, you're friends with the world's greatest cage-fighter? You must have some stories to tell,' Asias says and I glance into his starstruck eyes with a wry smile.

'Yup, conscripted to the same regiment. Me and Anguson were two peas in a pod – slumdogs from Medio with a history of street robbery. Given our size, no-one fucked with either of us. Even our superiors gave us an easy time,' I say.

'I bet Anguson was a real bad-ass in the military,' Asias says.

'You can say that again. Initially, we were sent to the streets of Lascao. Fuck, it was bloody. I saw Anguson's gun jam when he was face-to-face with an enemy. I couldn't shoot cause they were too close together. I watched Anguson disarm the fucker and place his thumbs into his eye sockets, then smash his skull into the ground. I doubt even the best cybernetics on the market can match Anguson for raw power. He's like nothing you've ever seen.'

Asias open his mouth and hesitates. 'I was gonna say I'd like to have seen that, but on second thoughts... I can't understand why Anguson didn't get a deferment, though.'

'I tried to get a fucking deferment.' Anguson booms, returning from the men's room and reclaiming his stool. 'Bastards said *No*. Forced me to put my career on hold, give up my lavish lifestyle. I thought about leaving Anatolia, but it became clear the war would follow me, and knowing those Elite bastards, they'd have frozen my assets, anyways.'

'On the plus side, Anguson somehow persuaded our superiors we'd be better suited to the navy. Got us stationed on the STS Cheriton. We thought it'd be a little easier, then we got hit by a fucking rocket. Ship sank, we made it to a lifeboat and were washed ashore in Nusantara. It's a miracle we survived, I doubt many others did,' I say.

'Enough of the depressing shit. These could be our final days and I want them to be cheerful. Asias, you're the only one who ever has anything positive to contribute. Tell us a happy story,' Anguson says.

'Er, I'm not sure I can tell a happy story,' Asias says.

'Course you can. I've seen the way your eyes glaze over when you talk about your family. Tell us the story of how you met your woman,' Anguson says.

'Where do I start? Ortellia was a girl who lived close by. I'd see her hanging out in the Fynhem district. Always thought she was out of my league, but I'd follow her around. I didn't know what to say so I'd yell her name or make fun of her and laugh with my friends. She couldn't stand me at first, even called me an obnoxious toad!

'One day I was beaten up by a gang and who was passing by? Ortellia. She screamed at them to stop. I swear she was ready to fight the bastards all by herself. They left me half-conscious in the alley and Ortellia helped me home, cleaned me up. We started talking. After that our friendship grew and eventually, ya know…

'She was always so lively, smiling. Everyone else in my life was so angry, but she was a shining light in a dark and miserable world.'

'Dark and miserable? You got that right,' Anguson says.

'Tell me about it. We've been fighting for the privilege of returning to a hell-hole. I can't believe I was taken in by those fucking Elites,' Asias says.

'Yeah, their tyranny almost makes me yearn for my childhood days,' I say.

'Why? Anatolia's always been a hell-hole,' Asias says.

'You probably don't remember the time before San Teria, but it was a little better, kind'a. In the noughties I wouldn't have believed things could get worse, but they did. After the election of twenty-sixteen, police brutality and mass incarceration became the norm, and half the country applauded this.

'Once upon a time, no-one thought an openly racist, sexist, homophobic, war-mongering candidate could win the Presidency, but Dyona Hildrem was a clever manipulator. She created common enemies for the people to unite against – immigrants, the poor, the non-religious – all treated as subhuman – all denied Citizenship in the new system. That's how bottom-levellers came to be.

'Of course, a bunch of stupid fuckers swore allegiance, faked piety, in order to gain Level Three Citizenship – turned out they had even less freedom than the bottom-levellers,' I say.

'Well, I guess I would be one of those stupid fuckers,' Asias says.

'I guess you were, and us who were rejected by the Elites were still called upon when they needed an army. Cheeky bastards forced us to join their ranks, swear allegiance or face the workcamp. And so we became members of a party we despised,' I say.

'And, of course, Hildrem became a victim of the poison she created. There's no doubt she was killed by her own party. Without a figurehead, San Teria became even less accountable,' James says.

'Okay, we're getting into the depressing shit again. Hey, July, why don't you strip for us?' Taiwo booms, rising from his seat, and the men cheer as the few women in the bar frown.

July grabs the bottom of her low-cut top, but Anguson snatches her wrist before she exposes her breasts and says: 'Keep your clothes on, baby.'

'Come on, Anguson, it's not like she's your woman,' Steve says.

'For the time being, she is,' Anguson says.

'You stupid bastard.' I sneer as Anguson wraps his arms around July's tiny waist. 'This is the problem with pleasure droids – their chips to emulate human behaviour make idiots like Anguson grow attached.'

'And then there's the artificial nerves to help them respond more naturally to touch, cater to our needs. Who needs a real wife when you can purchase one that looks better and never argues, eh Anguson?' Taiwo says.

'That's why you'll die a lonely man.' Asias laughs.

Necrosis

Locked in The Swine Inn for days on end, we watch war reports, talk about The Rebellion, sing and dance to noughties music, and laugh despite the constant tension. Non-guests sleep in the bar, on the floor, on chairs. A few dare to head home, despite the distant roar of gunfire and occasional rocket explosions. Others leave to join the Nusantaran army, wished luck by those who question if they will survive their journey through the streets, let alone be accepted. James provides free food and even free use of the pleasure droids to keep spirits high.

As the men watch a cage-fighting re-run on the big screen, Anguson escorts July to his bedroom. I head to the shower to refresh myself, feeling so fuzzy I can barely hold my eyelids open, or even hold a thought. The removal of my clothes is painful, and as I stand naked before the mirror, I can see necrosis consuming my arm and legs like an evil force. I can no longer move my toes or my right hand, and it occurs I may be dead soon.

I take a long, hot shower, and all I can think about is amputating my forearm and lowers legs, about what kind of freak I would become, no longer fully human, no longer in control – my artificial limbs malfunctioning whenever there is electromagnetic interference, or even just a loose wire.

I get dressed as painfully and clumsily as I got undressed, strapping my weapon and ammunition to my chest. Anguson roars from his bedroom so I cross the landing and knock, yelling: 'What's going on in there?' A minute later, the oaf opens the door, shirtless and red-faced as he buttons his trousers. July is lying naked on the bed; legs spread, pert titties pointing towards the ceiling.

'I'm sorry, was I a little rough?' July sits upright with multi-coloured hair hanging over her eyes. 'Please come back to bed.'

'Damn bitch malfunctioned, almost snapped off my fucking cock!'

I double over, laughing, but my laughs are feeble, wheezing, and I almost black out, leaning against the door-frame. Anguson puts on a shirt and then his holster, and as we head downstairs, pictures on the walls come to life. Sail ships rock in stormy seas as I fail to grab the banister, tumbling head-first, and everything fades…

DESTINY

I AWAKEN IN A SMALL, VAGUELY FAMILIAR ROOM, feeling dehydrated, eyelids barely open, limbs numb. The lighting is soft, diffused, but still hurts my eyes as I stare at the damaged ceiling tiles, glimpsing the cables above. Something is fixed to my mouth – a mask – and I can feel plastic tubes inside my nostrils. Wires are leading from my body to a machine at my bedside with an electronic screen. Something bad must have happened, but I have no memory.

I turn on my pillow to see Anguson's ragged red beard with brown roots showing. James and Asias are sitting beside the oaf, leaning forwards with their mouths agape. All three men are carrying guns in holsters, triggering memories of the Anatolian invasion. Was I collateral damage?

'I'll get the doc.' James rises from his plastic orange chair and leaves the room.

'So you're awake now?' Anguson says.

'What happened?' I murmur.

'You collapsed. Blood poisoning, apparently. We risked our lives to get you here. Drove through a bloody warzone. Twenty five thousand fucking credits this cost,' Anguson says.

'What do you mean?' I cough and the plastic tubes irritate my nostrils.

'Your surgery,' Anguson says.

'Oh shit.'

I jolt upright in my bed, staring at my right forearm which is now tubes of chrome with spherical hinges. I flex the artificial fingers, scarcely believing my mind has control over these *things*. I hold my real hand alongside my new one, wriggling fingers on both, controlling them with equal ease. They are pretty much the same size, apart from the flesh making my real hand slightly fatter.

'Best money can buy, in this country, anyways. And get this – no strength limiter. You're almost as strong as me now, in one arm, at least.' Anguson raises his eyebrows as though he expects gratitude, and then he laughs. The door opens and James enters with the doc who checks the electronic screen at my bedside. He removes the wires attached to my wrist and my chest by stickers, and then he removes the mask from my face.

'Two days you've been out,' the doc says. 'I had to amputate immediately. The necrosis was so extensive, there was no chance of saving your limbs, and if the blood poisoning worsened, it would've killed you. I had to drain every drop of blood from your body, replace it with coolant, clean it, and pump it back in. Your heart was stopped for one hour. Technically, you've come back from the dead.'

'Clean it? Does that mean I'm free of infection?' I say.

'Not quite. I injected a serum to cling to the toxins produced by the infection, and then I ran your blood through a centrifuge to separate the cells. This process will not have eradicated every microorganism, but I've given you a strong dose of medication.' The doc hands over a bottle of pills which I collect with my cybernetic hand. 'Take one of these a day. I'm not anticipating further problems from the infection, but you can expect to feel groggy, a little sore. I suggest resting for a week to recover.'

I remove the thin white blanket to see cybernetic legs attached to my knees, and I wriggle my metal toes. The doc points to my belongings on a bench and looks away as my belly hangs over my underpants. My feet clank on the cream tiles and I put on my clothes and holster, collect my weapon, and put the pills in my pocket.

'How do you feel?' Anguson says and the grogginess I felt moments ago is wearing off, fast.

'A little tired... Actually, no, I feel good. Surprisingly good. I feel... strong.'

We leave the secret office via a back door and follow dark corridors to a multi-storey car park containing few vehicles. We enter a car with a solar cell exterior and James removes a plug from a charging point then climbs into the driver's seat.

James slots a token into the machine at the exit barrier and we drive through the bleak streets of Batavia. We pass a huge pile of rubble with partially collapsed buildings either side. A store sign lies on the path and debris has spilt onto the road, making the ride bumpy. Guns roar in the distance and as they grow louder, James switches routes to avoid driving through crossfire.

We drive away from the roaring, heading in a large loop through the city, and I spot civilian vehicles just ahead – the first we have encountered. This makes me feel safer, but as the road curves we see a convoy of foot soldiers who stare into our windows, some glaring, some smiling. They allow our car to pass, but as the men shrink in the rearview mirror, a hot-headed soldier raises his rifle.

'Duck!' I yell, and then our back and front windows explode, sprinkling the seats with fragments of glass. I glance around the vehicle to see all three heads are miraculously intact. James floors the gas pedal, but Anguson demonstrates the same hot-headedness as his fellow countryman by returning fire. Our tyre explodes as we turn a bend at high speed and smash into a building; our bodies flying into airbags.

'Why the fuck did you open fire?' I say as we climb from the wreckage into an office with upturned desks and scattered papers. The car bonnet is covered in bricks and rubble, and the solar panels on the exterior are cracked. My joints ache and I momentarily fear my wiring has come loose, but I can fully control my cybernetics. Just as well.

'Self-defence, moron.' Anguson grunts, waving his KAL 10 as he emerges from the hole in the wall and scans the desolate high-street.

'Well, your self-defence has made us a target and we have to make it back on foot,' I say.

'In case you didn't notice, we were already a target,' Anguson says.

The four of us jog down the high-street, twitching and trembling as we peer around a corner for signs of military presence. Breaking cover, we reach a public square with a monument in the middle – knight on horseback at the pinnacle – and multi-storey streets forking off in every direction.

We rush past the steps of the monument and I hear loud gunfire, turning to see a soldier taking pot-shots from the end of a long road. Bullets chip pieces of white stone from the ornately-carved, towering column. Anguson fires pointlessly due to our KAL 10's limited range and the shutters of closed stores rattle.

I sprint towards a pedestrianised street of yellowish paving slabs and burgundy benches. My pace is extra-fast, each stride more like an antelope leap, so I slow to allow my friends time to catch up.

Asias and I run into an alley and I glance back to discover Anguson and James have gone the opposite way. The alley contains many gates and we could never reach the exit before the soldiers arrive so I whisper: 'You go into that gate. I'll go into this one. If need be, we can flank them.'

Asias follows my instruction so I enter a wooden gate and the creaking of the rusty hinges is excruciating. I stand in a yard between the gate and a wheelie bin; KAL 10 in my left hand, cybernetic hand ready to strike.

I hear noises close by, footsteps, shuffling, and my flesh and bone hand trembles. The temptation to burst through the gate and open fire is strong, but I maintain my composure, half-expecting these moments to be my last.

The noises louden and I get the sense the backyards are being checked by troops, fuck knows how many. I hear gunfire, loud, but not loud enough to be close by. Maybe Anguson and James are fighting Anatolian soldiers inside the other alley. Shit.

The gate opens and before my left index finger can pull the trigger, my cybernetic hand disarms my foe, then clamps on his throat. I carry him across the yard, legs kicking, and I slam his back against the wall, then I hear more gunfire – close this time. Saving ammunition, I tear out the soldier's throat, looking away as my cybernetic hand is soaked in blood.

I leap onto the seven-feet-high wall of the yard and from my vantage I see a pair of dead soldiers, but not Asias – he must be inside cover. I spot two soldiers hiding behind garbage cans and open fire, taking down the closest with a headshot. The furthest soldier breaks cover so I unload my machine pistol until both men lie dead in the gutter. Turning left, I see Asias had broken cover to assist, probably saving my worthless life.

I jump from the wall to grab an assault rifle in the gateway and Asias takes one from a dead man's grasp. Dual-wielding, we run along the alley, and as we reach the end, I am tossed by a deafening explosion; my limp body skidding along the ground.

Dazed, I get to my cybernetic feet and flex my fingers to confirm they are functioning, but my relief is short-lived as I spot Asias lying below a collapsed wall; half his face red and black. I approach slowly and tearily to discover the young man I thought was a corpse is still breathing. Just. His eyes roll in my direction as he whimpers, trying to speak, and I remove the bricks, sharing the agony of every burn and fracture.

'Leo, I-I need you to find my wife...' Asias gasps, barely clinging to life as I brush the rubble from his chest. 'She's in Medio Level Three... Ortellia... Basilides... Tell her I love her... that she's the light of my...'

I fix Asias' gaze and the whites of his eyes are now grey, bulging; his charred complexion shrouded by a dust cloud.

'Tell her to tell my son, Arturo... to tell him... I'm sorry... that Daddy's proud of him... that I'll always be watching... tell him to always believe in himself, to find a way out, to make a better life... tell him Daddy believes in...'

Asias trembles, his head slumps onto rubble, and I reach out to shake his motionless body, but I stop my hands midway. 'Asias! Asias! Wake up, damn it...'

I stare at his half-burnt face, broad nose and lips, short beard – a less ugly version of me, no more than twenty years old with eyeballs rolled upwards. Tears drip onto the rubble as my friend dies in a foreign land with no prospect of burial. I look to the swirling grey clouds, resisting the urge to roar, and then I lower my gaze, wheezing.

'I'll find them, Asias, make sure they're okay. I'll tell them everything you said... I promise.'

I wipe my brow with my trembling wrist and spin my head as I hear clanking footsteps. As I rise to my cybernetic feet, a mechanoid emerges at the top of the alley – a bipedal mass of yellow armour plates and weaponised arms designed for one purpose – to kill.

In my fury, I charge at the mechanoid, pouncing as its gun-arms rise, and staring into the eyes of the pilot as I latch onto its one vulnerability – its chest-plate. Pressing my feet against its groin area, I pull so hard my cybernetic arm almost separates from its fleshy stump. The chest-plate comes off and I tear into the wiring as the mechanoid trembles and becomes still, neutralised with the pilot helpless in the cockpit.

Two soldiers open fire from behind the mechanoid, bullets precipitating against its shell. I leap over the gunfire, reaching the first of my foes in two bounds and flinging him into his comrade. Both bodies skid into a charge point for electrical vehicles.

I run towards a four-storey building, leap to a first-floor windowsill, squeeze my toes between sandstone bricks, leap to the next window, repeat and repeat again, reaching the roof-ledge and climbing on top of the building where the wind is stronger.

From my vantage, I see a convoy of soldiers many blocks away, but nothing closer, so I leap from rooftop to rooftop, heading in what I assume is the direction of The Swine Inn.

A large gap appears and a multi-storey car-park stands opposite, taller than most surrounding buildings. Taking many steps back, I run and leap the width of the road and pavements, landing on the fourth floor of the car-park. I kick open the door to a staircase and spiral to the top level, from where I take in the full spectacle of Batavia – the sky-scraping towers of glass, the statue of the Jebedan God Ceros, the football stadium, the parkland that lies beyond the river.

Descending the stairs, I bound through the streets like an antelope, past a patrol of soldiers before they can react, entering an alley, leaping to a fire escape, clanking to the top level and leaping between roofs again, shuffling down a drainpipe near the town square where the magnificent Ceros stands.

As I reach the flawless white slabs, a light streaks from the sky and an explosion knocks me to the ground. The sound is deafening, agonising. I sit up to see the five-chain tall statue tilting, gaining speed and plummeting face-down; the sword breaking from the hand as white slabs ripple and crack, my eardrums bursting a second time. A convoy approaches the calamity so I leap onto the neck of the statue, taking cover behind the rhinoceros head until the men pass.

Sliding from the bicep of the statue, I run through the streets and down the embankment; my strides huge due to the gradient. As I reach the swing-bridge, I discover it has been struck by a rocket and each broken half is part-submerged. I grip the handrail and descend the sloping bridge, splashing into the debris-filled river.

I swim past a severed human head and bump into a torso, gasping and swallowing filthy water. Grabbing the handrail, I climb from the river and scale the broken bridge, entering the streets of the embankment. I reach

The Swine Inn, banging on the doors and gasping with a stronger sense of exhaustion than I have ever felt. An exhaustion exacerbated by the dread of the news I must break.

'It's Leo, open up,' I yell and the door is opened by one of the bar staff who has not returned home since the invasion. I enter the establishment, water dripping from my stooped head as I stand among armed deserters. Faces wilt in response to my distress and I feel reluctant to say what no-one wants to hear.

'We were at-attacked, separated from Anguson and James. Asias is dead.'

THE RETURN TO ANATOLIA

ANGUSON AND JAMES RETURN TO THE SWINE INN, unharmed, but sweating profusely; their gun hands twitching, eyes bulging like rookie soldiers on the battlefield for the first time. I have never seen the former world champion appear so weak, shivering, traumatised by the actions of his compatriots. And then the thought occurs, Anguson and I have killed civilians too.

'Fucking bastards were killing for fun,' James whimpers with hands on knees, then he stands straight and roars: 'Our fellow fucking countrymen!'

'We tried to help, killed a bunch of 'em, managed to disappear in the ensuing carnage… Where's Asias?' Anguson's gaze shifts around the bar.

'He didn't make it. I'm sorry,' I whisper as grief-stricken faces loom.

'You mean he's…' James lowers his pink eyes, trembling.

'Wife and kid – baby. I promised I'd pass on a message before he…' My voice breaks and I bite my lips until they hurt. 'All I know is they live in a Level Three area of Medio, but I'll find them, help with money if I can.'

James sits silently behind the bar for minutes, then fills a half-pint glass with vodka which he downs in three gulps.

'He was a good lad, Asias. Just nineteen years old, I believe, but I could see his potential.' James' eyes glaze over with a hint of pride in the sadness. 'I had high hopes of him rising through the ranks of the Rebellion, growing into a leader. He was smart, ya know. Not many young lads can hold a conversation about something other than girls and football, but he was different.'

'So often, he was the voice of reason. When grown men were behaving like boys, he was the man in the room,' Taiwo says.

'And just like that, he's gone…' Steve punches the table, curling his lips as an empty glass rolls onto the floor and smashes. Nobody picks up the pieces.

We continue the talk about the loss of Asias, the family he left behind, and fury simmers within the despondent room; the sense of tragedy reflected in the teary eyes of ex-soldiers. One woman says a prayer and although few here are religious, we all share the sentiment. Some of the men are determined to seek vengeance and a group of eleven leave to join the Nusantaran army. Three others take the risk of heading to the airport with no clue as to whether flights are grounded; their argument being that we are sitting ducks and must get out before Batavia is reduced to rubble. The loudness and frequency of explosions suggest that process will not take long.

Over the coming days, the news on the big screen shows a huge push by the Nusantaran army and they appear to have retaken much of the capital. This only brings the fear of an anti-matter strike.

On the positive side, my infection has cleared and I feel much better, physically speaking, but it occurs Asias only lost his life to save mine, and I feel guilty that thought had not occurred sooner.

The time until our flight passes in a drunken blur as we drain James' alcohol supply and enjoy every pleasure droid, bar one. The men are keen to test the Jane Apolinario lookalike, but Anguson does not allow so much as a titty flash, which is probably better for everyone's safety. Finally, the day arrives for us to leave Nusantara and the cage-fighter approaches his favourite doll at the bar.

'July baby, I have to go now. These last few weeks have been great. Well, hell on Eryx really, but ya know what I'm saying. You've made the misery bearable–'

'Fucking hell, are you making a speech?' I say incredulously and Anguson glares; his nostrils flaring. 'Is that a tear in your eye? It is, isn't it?'

'You'll have to stay with James now. I'll miss you, baby.'

A tear rolls down July's cheek and Anguson kisses her affectionately, then squeezes her arse with both hands. The lovebirds hug as I turn to the approaching James Jones who has emerged from behind the bar. He fixes my gaze with grey eyes which soften an otherwise hard face, like a block of granite with deep lines etched into its surface.

'It's been a journey, friend. Thanks for everything you've done.'

'It's been my pleasure, Leo, and I expect we haven't seen the last of one another. I've arranged for you to be picked up when you land. A guy called Hitchens will be waiting at the airport. He'll be wearing a top with triple X on the front. He'll take you to the Rebellion's office in Underworld. And then you two can help overthrow those San Terian bastards.'

Anguson and I say our goodbyes to every man and woman, and Erica rushes over to give me a hug, much to my embarrassment. We remove our contact lenses from their packaging in order to deceive the eye scanner in the airport. I place the lenses onto my eyeballs and blink a few times, then laugh as Anguson struggles to do the same. One of the rebels leads us out the back of The Swine Inn and drives us to the airport in a saloon car.

'Why would you risk your life to transport us through the city?' I say.

'We'll be risking our lives everyday for the cause. And I don't know about you, but I refuse to cower from my own damn people,' our driver says, unflinchingly.

'Well, the gesture's appreciated.' I nervously scan the streets, relieved by the emerging sight of Nusantaran uniforms. We progress unimpeded to discover Batavia is high on military presence and low on conflict, but the cityscape is now barely recognisable. Glass towers bear gaping holes, stone buildings have been reduced to rubble, and the statue of Ceros is lying face-down in the fractured town square.

At 7:15pm, we reach the airport which is heavily guarded and fully operational with many people entering, but none leaving. We have arrived several hours before take-off because we are unsure of check-in time and cannot afford to miss this flight. The last of our remins are squandered at the bar as we await the arrival of midnight. Holding glasses to our mouths, we watch every passing cop in fear they are coming to apprehend the Anatolians in their airport.

We stand tensely in a queue as departure time arrives, yet the false travel document of Sydney Anguson fails to raise an eyebrow. A security guard hurriedly scans our eyes and fingers with a handheld device and lets us pass through customs.

As we ride the boarding bus, I admire the nearby scramjet – a black arrow with a huge inlet below the cockpit which sucks in air for the turbine engine.

We depart the boarding bus, climb the airstair, and follow the aisle to our seats, putting our bags in overhead lockers and sighing as we fasten our seatbelts. The scramjet flies into the stratosphere where the stars are clear and the clouds below are lit by explosions.

We cross the black Aral Sea from Nusantara to Nyberu and I admire a coastal city from the edge of space. I gulp as blinding light is followed by the formation of a mushroom cloud and two colossal concentric rings.

As I blink tears from my eyes, the aisles of the scramjet fall silent and the city lights are no more…

Millions of vapourised humans linger in the sky as we soar at hypersonic speed. And my face remains pressed against the window long after the mushroom cloud is out of sight.

Numbed and muted, we cross two wartorn continents in a couple of hours, landing safely in the neutral territory of Scania. The tension is high in one of the last havens on Eryx. And I wonder whether it would be best to disappear here, but neutrality will count for nothing if the victor continues the destruction.

HOME SOIL

FOR THREE DAYS, we wait in Gamla Stan airport, broke, hungry, and forced to drink from bathroom taps until we catch our next flight, crossing the vast and cold Barbeton Ocean which is filled with warships.

The scramjet lands in Anatolia and we venture into Gaeliao airport, finding a man with XXX on his top. He is maybe forty-five years old and broad-boned with greying hair and thin, chapped lips. I approach as he strums his foot below a directional sign. 'Hitchens?'

'Follow me,' Hitchens says in a coarse voice, abruptly turning and marching out of the airport which is just as packed with armed guards as the one in Batavia. We are led into the carpark where a maglev car awaits – a hybrid vehicle with wheels for standard driving and magnetic levitation technology for modern highways. The body is long and sleek, bearing photovoltaic panels to convert sunlight into horsepower. We climb into leather seats in the rear, and as Hitchens starts the vehicle, seat-belts slide across our bodies, automatically locking in place.

'Take us to Medio city,' Hitchens instructs and an electronic voice replies: *'Length of journey, one thousand, one hundred and eleven miles. Estimated arrival time six-twenty-four pm.'*

'Eight fucking hours,' Anguson mutters. 'I just want a bed. Is that too much to ask?'

'Stop yapping and get your head down if you're so tired,' I say.

'Can't fucking sleep upright,' Anguson mumbles, shuffling in his seat as we leave the carpark and cruise through an unfamiliar city.

The pedestrians on their daily routines almost make wartime seem mundane, but there is a noticeable absence of young men on the streets. A large banner waves from the facade of a public building, reading: *Victory is Nigh!* The claim seems unlikely, given the bloodiness of the fighting, but the Citizens of Anatolia will swallow any propaganda.

Our vehicle meets the slip-road of a maglev highway and hovers a couple of feet high as its wheels retract. We whizz at double speed over a red metal grid with repulsive barriers to stop vehicles veering off-road.

The highway rises above the slums and our elevation reveals a cityscape just a few miles across, located in a desert with mountains on the horizon. Hitchens switches on the radio and says: 'The door compartments contain food and water.' Anguson and I immediately delve into mini-fridges, removing bottled water and packaged sandwiches. We stuff our faces, finishing our second sandwiches as we reach the city outskirts and return to ground level.

'You guys must've had an interesting time out there?' Hitchens' seat swivels to face backwards as I gulp my water.

'You mean surviving a shipwreck? Spending weeks at sea? Living off coconuts and shellfish when we hit dry land? Grafting on a rice farm? Resorting to armed robbery? Getting shot? Losing an arm and leg? Seeing a good friend killed by a mech? Yeah, interesting.' I sigh.

'You forgot to mention I lost the love of my life.'

'Oh yeah, and Anguson fell in love with a pleasure droid.'

'Sydney fucking Anguson – the world's greatest cage-fighter resorting to fucking rubber dolls.' Hitchens laughs.

'It was either that or Jardine's arse. I think I made the right choice,' Anguson says.

'Seems like six and two threes from where I'm sitting.' Hitchens stares at my new arm. 'I see you have some nice cybernetics there, my friend.'

'Certainly not through choice. I've never been a fan of augmentation, but I must admit, now I've got them, I feel, well, powerful. Suddenly I understand the appeal,' I say.

'Powerful, eh? I take it there's no strength limiter?' Hitchens says.

'Nope, I tore a soldier's throat clean out during the invasion. And my running speed, damn, I can go fast now. At least twice as fast as before and I can leap three, maybe four times higher.'

'Perfect soldier material,' Hitchens says.

'He's still not as tough as me, though. No fucker can handle Sydney Anguson.'

'Settle down, Princess, your role will be strictly office-based. We can't have a celebrity breaking a fingernail on the battlefield,' Hitchens says.

'Hey, cheeky fucker, I've seen more frontline action than most. I'm no princess,' Anguson says.

'Relax, I was just kidding.' Hitchens' laughter is obscured by the roar of passing fighter jets. 'You men ready for this?'

'The Rebellion? We're more than ready. San Teria left us with nothing to lose. The sooner we overthrow the bastards, the better,' I say as we whizz by a crater in the desert, surrounded by charcoal houses and windowless towers. A once-thriving area is no longer populated, even by insect-life, and I can feel my cancer-risk increasing with every passing second.

'That was Lilesa city. Fucking nuke. A million dead. People blame the enemy, but there can be no doubt San Teria brought this upon us. The only way to stop more destruction is to put ourselves in harm's way.

'We have several sites designated for bombing, and no, the irony is not lost on me. Given the high presence of the San Terian Guard, this could mean shootouts, death, imprisonment. The Rebellion will be no easy ride,' Hitchens says.

'What's a city with a few San Terian Guards compared to a jungle with lead flying everywhere, mines below our feet, and fire raining from the sky? This shit will be a walk in the park,' I say.

'Well, some of it will be. Much of our efforts revolve around cyber-terrorism which is obviously safer,' Hitchens says.

'We'll reserve that role for Princess Anguson.' I smirk as we climb a steep and winding road at the edge of the mountain range. Our vantage offers the spectacular sight of pine forests and misty valleys – the roaming ground of mutants created by the last nuclear war. Anatolia is so vast that ninety percent of the land is wilderness, half forested areas where creatures are evolving at such a rate, you never know what to expect. New species are documented on an almost daily basis.

'Fuck you, Jardine,' Anguson mutters after a short silence.

'So, are *you* okay with all of this?' Hitchens says.

'Sure I am. It's not like we can shy away from killing – it's a necessary part of life – as natural to men as to lions,' Anguson says.

'Without violence, the good things just aren't possible. We should be respectful about our victims, yes, but not hypocritical, not hesitant about what we must do. This is about survival at all costs,' I say.

'Spoken like true lions... I'm not sure I believe violence is a necessary part of life so much as a necessary part of today. You two sound even more cynical than I do. Life must've fucked you up real good,' Hitchens says.

'To be honest, I was a bastard from the start – typical bully – but I suppose I was good to friends,' Anguson says.

'You've never struck me as a bully. Idiot? *Yes*. Loose-cannon? *Sometimes...*' I say and Anguson crinkles his brow, then looks to Hitchens.

'To be honest, I didn't like who I was, scaring the crap out of people – kids as desperate as me. Shit, I wanted to change, but I soon I realised this is hardwired into me. I go from one form of violence to another, and the fucked up thing is, it's all I'm good for,' Anguson says.

'You almost make yourself sound like a monster, but I see more than *that*. Monsters can emerge within us all, but something creates them. What created yours?' Hitchens says.

'Well, my father used to beat the crap out of me and my sister until I started growing up. By the age of thirteen I was as big as him and socked it to the fucker. Knocked him out cold.

'Me and Luka went to live on the streets. I always wanted to take care of her, but that manifested itself as controlling her every move. Eventually, we went our separate ways. I saw her a couple of years back; she spoke to me like a stranger. And who can blame her? I keep telling myself, telling others I'm one of the good guys, but my track record says otherwise.'

'Your remorse shows you're better than many and your eagerness to join the cause shows you seek redemption,' Hitchens says.

'Redemption? Yeah, I need to earn that. Back in Batavia, I shot a fucking civilian. We were robbing his store for the money to get home. Poor bastard pulled on us. In all my years of street robbery, I never killed, and then as a grown man, as a reformed character, I did just that and acted like it was okay,' Anguson says.

'But the killing was out of desperation. Your victim was a victim of war, and I hate to say this, but there will be more of those victims. You're not going to fall apart on us, are you?' Hitchens says.

'Like I said, violence is all I'm good for.' Anguson turns up his nose and the sadness in his eyes suggests he does not believe his own words.

'So what got Sydney Anguson into cage-fighting?' Hitchens bears a smile which jars with the current mood.

'After a few years of robbery, I decided to walk a different path, thought I'd start earning, rather than taking, so I visited the underground Fight Club at Titan Stolastic. I kept beating grown men at sixteen years of age. Sure, I lost one or two times, but I was still a kid. Anyways, my reputation grew and a promoter signed me up to the professional ranks.'

Hitchens gives an impressed nod and says: 'And that's how a legend was born…'

Pines give way to flat land and a megalopolis comes into view with three colossal towers at its centre, each of them two miles high and gleaming white. San Teria's trillion credit masterpiece, known as Skye City, is the focal point of Medio – the untouched capital of Anatolia, guarded by an anti-missile system not afforded to poorer cities. The twenty five million non-Citizens at the Elites' feet, scornfully referred to as 'bottom-levellers', are not so fortunate, and blast craters are visible in hillside slums. Given that no nuclear warheads have made it through the net, I suspect these smaller breaches are no accident.

'You'd think San Teria would allocate all resources to the war, but get this, we've uncovered plans to link those towers via three huge plateaus, and here's where it gets really crazy: they're gonna build an elevator to that space-station they keep showing on the news. You ever heard anything so bizarre?' Hitchens says.

'I'll believe it when I see it,' I mutter, envisioning the absurdity of an elevator reaching into space.

We cruise by the toxic river Tinanmoue and enter the industrialised outskirts of Medio city. The maglev highway leads above factories and slums, and through the outer- and inner-hubs of the city proper where only registered Citizens are allowed to roam.

At the end of the maglev highway, the vehicle lands on its wheels and we follow a crumbling road in manual drive. We cross a wasteland, breaching a hole in a wire-mesh fence which leads onto unused railway lines.

As we enter an abandoned tunnel network, the headlights unveil graffiti-covered walls. Hitchens steers up a narrow ramp and parks on what was once a train platform, but is now something less welcoming. Beyond the parked vehicles are iron shacks, workbenches, contraptions, and men working to heavy metal music. Candles are the only lightsources and the sneering faces revealed by flickering flames create a hellish vibe. This place is known as Underworld – a subterranean city for gangsters, ex-cons, and fugitives.

On foot, we venture through the shacks, then climb an inactive escalator, follow a curving corridor of panelled walls, and enter a doorway with a sign which reads: *Westgate Mall.*

We pass stores run by crooks, ascend another escalator, navigate junk on the oil-stained floor, and arrive at a blacked-out window bearing a skull and crossbones. Hitchens enters a code on a panel to open an iron door, saying: 'Welcome to your new home.'

Underworld

We stand inside a cavernous room which contains workbenches, a circular saw, tools, raw materials, and electronic devices. Lightbulbs and a chain with a hook are hanging from ceiling rigging which is entangled with wires. People are working in greasy overalls and one lifts a welding mask to reveal a blotchy face with a wide mouth and pointed nose. Her body language is masculine with sharp, forceful movements, legs wide apart, and chin held aloft.

'Hello Nyota, these are the new recruits – Leo Jardine and–'

'Sydney Anguson,' Nyota interrupts.

'I'll be signing autographs later. Right now, I need sleep.' Anguson smirks and Nyota glares until his expression fades.

'You may be a celebrity out there, Mister, but in here, you're just another grunt, and you'll be expected to pull your weight.'

'Get him told, Nyota.' Hitchens chuckles.

'Freedom fighting isn't all glamorous; we need to fund operations so you'll be expected to graft – fifty hours a week. Oh, and we know you have deep pockets; we'll need to delve into them from time-to-time. You don't like it, feel free to return to the other side,' Nyota says.

'What price freedom, right?' Anguson shrugs.

'Come on, men, I'll show you around,' Hitchens says.

Nyota closes her mask and sparks fly from her welding iron as she resumes her work, and I cannot deny having a little crush on her. Hitchens leads us through the workroom into a corridor with bad lighting and walls that are blue at the bottom and grey at the top. '*This* is my office. No-one enters without knocking.' Hitchens points to the varnished door of his office, then leads into a different room which is pitch black inside. He flicks the light switch to reveal a long metal table with a holographic projector in the centre.

Unlike the workshop, this area is basic and tidy with a grey carpet, grey walls, and a grey ceiling. Hitchens points to one of three barely visible hatches and says: 'There are holoscreens fixed into the walls. They'll emerge if you call them by number like this: *Holoscreen One, activate.*' A hatch opens and a holoscreen emerges with a solar system screensaver which looks three-dimensional, despite being displayed on a flat surface.

'Just pull up a chair whenever you need to work. We'll be training you to become hackers among other things. Oh, and you can switch to the security camera view like this: *Security Camera One.*' The holoscreen displays the dark entrance tunnel with the train tracks. '*Security Camera Nine.*' The holoscreen displays men working in candle light on the train platform.

'Security is essential. We need to be ready at all times. We have gun turrets and other security devices, but we mustn't depend on them. Keep your wits about you, and always err on the side of caution.' Hitchens approaches a steel cabinet and removes two holowatches, handing one to each of us. I strap my holowatch around my left wrist and Anguson does the same. 'There's a list of contacts in the holowatch address book. I'll go through them later, but if ever you're in trouble, any of these people will help.'

Hitchens deactivates the holoscreen and leads us into another room with a long metal table, holographic projector, and metal cabinets. Chrome weapons cover the hole-filled walls – rifles, pistols, and phasers mounted on hooks. Anguson peruses the collection and I could swear there is a bulge in his pants.

'This is the armoury. Nothing is locked up in case we need quick access. Ammo and grenades can be found in the cabinets, but the weapons are fully loaded so no playing with them,' Hitchens says.

'If anyone invaded this place, it'd be a bloodbath,' I mutter.

'That's the aim.' Hitchens leads out the door and points towards a lobby in the glow of a lampshade with flower-shaped holes. '*That's* the kitchen. The next room is the showers, and that door *there* is the emergency exit.'

Hitchens presses down on a creaky door handle and backs into cramped, smelly sleeping quarters which contain eight bunks and eight lockers. Most of the beds bear ruffled blankets, strewn clothes, and tablet computers ten years out of date. Anguson dumps his luggage on the floor and removes his shoes to climb into one of the tidy bunks. The oaf is snoring within seconds so I shrug at Hitchens and mumble: 'May as well do the same, I'm exhausted.'

'That bunk *there* is unoccupied. Anguson is sleeping in Nyota's bunk, and I wouldn't like to be him when she finds out. Get your head down. I'll see you in the morning.'

NEW BEGINNINGS

DURING THE NIGHT, I hear Nyota yelling at Anguson, and bury my head under the pillow to return to my dream. What seems like minutes later, Hitchens yells: 'Men, it's time to get up,' and I awaken to discover Anguson sleeping in a different bunk.

The lack of windows or a clock inside this humid chamber means I cannot gauge the time as I rise from my pit. We gather in the kitchen for breakfast, too sleepy for introductions or small talk, and then we shower and change into blue overalls.

Hitchens leads us into the workroom and demonstrates his engineering skills as Nyota issues orders to the men. We spend the entire day learning how to repair electronic devices for resale with little talk of the Rebellion. Anguson's thick fingers struggle to master control of the soldering iron and wire clippers, but my cybernetic hand makes the work a cinch.

'So Hitchens, how'd you end up in this lovely part of the world?' Anguson says, late in the afternoon.

'Ex-special forces, defector like you,' Hitchens says without looking up as he wires a circuit board. 'Spent time in prison for assaulting a superior officer. Punched the fucker right in the nose then beat him into unconsciousness.'

'And what did he do to deserve that? Anguson laughs.

'Wanted us to massacre civilians. We found families cowering inside an old building, disobeyed a direct order to gun them down. Apparently women and children posed a direct threat, fucking bastards. Anyways, I was court-martialled, served a few years inside, escaped, ended up here.'

'Fucking hell, how'd you escape?' Anguson says and Hitchens downs his soldering iron to make eye contact.

'Stupid bastards underestimated a marine. I knocked a guard out cold, tied him up in my cell, took his uniform and weapon, and casually walked out. The security was abysmal.'

'Sounds like it... So we're not the only ones who've gone to extraordinary lengths to be here...' Anguson grins.

'I can confirm that down here, you two are completely unremarkable.'

Hitchens collects a wheelbarrow from the corner and boxes up some of our products, placing them inside, and filling two more wheelbarrows. A handle grates against my cybernetic hand as we push them through Westgate Mall, passing many stores with skulls and demons in the windows. Underworld could really use a feminine touch.

The lack of ventilation means the air is thick and stale, and every step makes me increasingly breathless. Broken lights spark as we enter a store where shelves are overstocked with electronic devices not dissimilar to our wares. We approach a wooden bench where a merchant is sitting with metal fangs, and Hitchens says: 'Shep, how's it going?' in a loud and jovial manner.

'As miserable as ever. Barely made a sale all day. Been fending off chancers haggling for lower prices than I paid for this shit.'

'Well, I have the solution to your problems – top quality merchandise. Should sell out within hours,' Hitchens says.

'Okay, Hitch, show me what you've got.' Shep sighs, walking around his bench for a better view of our supplies.

'An Emstrad two-thousand-six-hundred, a Duraton holocamera, an XLK laser alarm...' Hitchens raises items from the wheelbarrows, one-by-one. 'The entire stock is yours for fifteen hundred credits.'

Shep looks to the speckled ceiling tiles and laughs with his hands on his hips. 'I'm afraid you're gonna have to lower your asking price. I'll give you eight hundred for the lot.'

'Are you kidding me? A lot of work has gone into this shit. I can go to twelve hundred, and only because you're a good client,' Hitchens says.

'Make it eleven hundred and you have a deal.'

Hitchens stares impatiently into Shep's red eyes and then the men firmly shake hands. Shep removes the money from his till and counts out twenty-two fifty credit notes on the bench. Hitchens collects the money and stuffs it into the front pocket of his overalls, clicking the popper-button. We carry the merchandise into a poorly-stocked storage room, placing items into boxes and onto shelves.

'Before we return to the office, I need to collect a debt. Having you two with me should make that a whole lot easier.'

We head to the train platform with our empty wheelbarrows and Hitchens approaches a man tinkering with a motorbike engine. 'Cooper, I need a word.' Hitchens snarls and as the pair discuss money, I spot a shirtless man sitting at a bench, tattooing his forearm. His torso is covered in high-quality ink, and if this body art is comparable to his own handiwork, I am seriously impressed.

Anguson stands shoulder to shoulder with Hitchens as I approach the tattooist and say: 'Any chance I can get a tattoo when you're done?'

'Depends on what you want,' the tattooist says without looking away from his needle.

'Oh, it's nice and simple. I just want the letters A.S.T.R. tattooed on my forearm.'

'Come to see me at seven on Friday. It'll be one hundred credits.'

Hitchens successfully collects his debt after a vigorous discussion and we return to the office in the mall. We microwave ready-meals, collect fruit from a bowl, and eat in the sleeping quarters, then Anguson and I climb into our bunks. Fucking jet lag. Our week continues in the same repetitive manner and I wonder if the insurrection will ever get underway. I want to overthrow San Teria yesterday.

On Friday, I get paid two hundred credits for my labour and return to the tattooist at 7:00pm. I sit at his workbench as he shows a list of lettering styles and I choose one similar to that of Asias' tattoo. We get started without a stencil and as the needle meets my forearm, it prompts belated hygiene concerns, but this symbolism matters more than my health.

'So what does A.S.T.R. stand for?' the tattooist says over the hum of the needle.

'You don't know?' I say.

'How the hell would I know?' The tattooist shakes his head and his nose-ring reflects the candlelight.

'Oh, I just assumed, er, never mind. I probably shouldn't say – it's kind'a personal to me. I lost a friend with the same tattoo so it's a tribute to him, but it's more than that,' I say.

'More than that?' that tattooist says.

'I suppose it signifies a fresh start, new beginnings.'

'Fresh start in this hell hole? You're not high, are you?' The tattooist crumples his brow.

'No, just optimistic.' I laugh.

'When we're done, give me some of whatever you're smoking. Good gear is hard to come by these days.'

Humidity rises as the men labour on the train platform, tinkering with their engines, and one hour of stinging and wincing slowly passes. When my A.S.T.R. tattoo is complete, I admire the green lettering on my inflamed skin – this freehand effort is truly a thing of beauty. Suddenly, I feel intrinsically connected to the cause, to my lost friend. The Rebellion is part of me now.

The tattooist removes a bandage from sterile packaging, wraps my forearm, and says: 'Leave the dressing on for a minimum of twenty four hours.' I pay the one hundred credit fee and return to our headquarters with a permanent reminder of what I am fighting for.

A Glimpse of the Future

I spend my evenings at the holoscreen, drinking coffee, but online research fails to yield clues as to the whereabouts of Bilton's sister, Mary. Given that I have virtually nothing to go on, this comes as no surprise, but the guilt intensifies, night by night, and the horror of cannibalism haunts my nightmares. The half-eaten corpse of Bilton taunting, jeering, roaring until I wake in cold sweats…

My other targets have not been so difficult to locate, given the unusual names of mother and child, and the fact the Rebellion have unauthorised access to San Teria's Citizen database. Giving up hope on Mary, I leave Underworld to make the most nerve-racking journey since my first descent into battle.

A rocket explodes in the sky as I ride a motorbike along the disused railway lines on a cold and breezy morning. I reach the Fynhem district and every drug fiend I pass provokes a flashback to the misery of my youth, the wretches I survived among, who I could so easily have become. I shudder at the thought – not that PTSD and alcoholism are any better.

A set of towers dominate a Level Three neighbourhood; social housing blocks that stretch twenty five stories high like stacked prison cells. The windows are near-black with grime, and extensive damp patches are causing cracks in the crimson walls.

At the intercom of a tower, I press *seven* and *nine* followed by a bell symbol, and a moment later a female whispers: 'Hello.'

'Hello, I'm looking for a lady named Ortellia.' I am met by silence. 'I'm a friend of Asias, or I was…'

A buzzing is followed by a click of the lock so I open a door of reinforced iron and enter the premises. I approach an elevator and hit the summon button, but the floor lights remain inactive. A few minutes of waiting confirm no elevator is coming so I ascend the many stairs, wondering how the hell a mother would manage this climb with a baby. The stairwell stinks due to bin-bags dumped by those who lack the energy to reach the garbage cans outside.

I pass teenagers playing rap music, reaching the relevant floor and knocking at a door coated in chipped blue paint. A moment later, the door opens, but the chain remains in place as a woman peers through the gap. Her face is pretty despite her baggy eyes, dry skin paler than her husband's, and long, unbrushed, brunette hair.

'Hello, are you Ortellia?'

'Y-yes.'

'My name is Leo Jardine. I don't know whether you've been told, but…' I hesitate, trembling, and Ortellia interrupts:

'He's dead, killed on the battlefield. They told me months ago.'

'That's not entirely accurate. I was with Asias when he… May I come in.'

Ortellia unlocks the door and stoops her head as she shuffles into a front room with no windows. A picture of Asias in military uniform is hanging from a mouldy wall – he seems so young, so proud, and far from ready for his coming Hell. The furnishings consist of two brown two-seater couches, a compuscreen, a stove, and not much else. We sit on opposite seats and I play nervously with my thumbs.

'It's good to meet you at last. Your husband spoke about you often – all good things.'

'What is it that you want?' Ortellia asks without looking up; her skinny frame swamped in a cream, cotton dress, her body language broken.

'I came to tell you, er…' I take a deep breath. 'Your husband, Asias, he didn't die on the battlefield. He, myself, and many others realised we were fighting an unjust war and sought refuge in Nusantara. Asias was too ashamed to tell you, but he had no reason to be ashamed. He was one of the bravest men I've ever met, although he was scarred by what he'd seen.'

Ortellia opens her mouth, lips trembling, but words fail to emerge so I continue:

'I probably shouldn't say this, but I feel you should know: We were planning a revolution to overthrow the government. We still are. It was thanks to your husband I joined the cause – and his loss gives me extra motivation to succeed. I don't know what you think about San Ter–'

'I hate them,' Ortellia says robotically.

'Me too. It's a shame Asias didn't… Your husband spoke every day about you, about his son, about how he wanted to make a difference. He told me to say that you're the light of his life, that he's sorry for leaving you.'

'How did he…'

'Anatolia invaded Nusantara. I fell sick, lapsed into a coma and was taken for treatment. Asias was escorting me from surgery, but we were attacked upon our return. There was a rocket blast. Asias was badly injured. He spoke about you and his son with his dying breath. He had a message for Arturo. Is he here?'

'He's in the other room, through *that* door.' Ortellia points, then looks down as tears pour from her eyes.

I nod and curl my lips, then climb from the sofa to enter a bedroom as barren as the living room. The boy is tucked under a blanket on a mattress with no base, lying perfectly calm but wide awake. His face is the image of his father's, but a lighter shade of brown due to the maternal bloodline. He can be no more than nine months old, but he fixes my gaze with a confidence, with flames burning in his eyes, as though he is staring into my soul. And I know immediately what Asias meant – this boy is special.

'Hi, little guy, I'm a friend of your father's, or at least I was. I'm sad to say he is no longer with us, but I'm here today to fulfil a promise to him. I only knew Asias a short time, but he made an impression on me. I've no doubt he would've made a great father. All he did was speak about how proud he was of you, about how he wanted to make this world a better place for you to grow up.

'He was a young man, but he was strong, brave. He was gonna help us overthrow our corrupt leaders. He had a tattoo on his arm.' I roll up the sleeve of my flesh and bone arm. 'I've got one to match, now. It has the letters A.S.T.R. It stands for Alliance of San Terian Renegades. You won't understand the significance of this yet, but our nation is ruled by an evil party called San Teria who are trying to take over the world. They force Citizens to swear allegiance to them. That's where the word *renegade* comes in – it means a person who has changed allegiance.

'I am going to fight for the cause your father believed in, and others are going to help me. I was with Asias at the end and he wanted me to tell you to always believe in yourself and that he'll always be watching. He said you must find a way out, make a better life for yourself, and I am determined that our revolution will make that process easier for you and for children like you.

'Your father said you were different, special, and that he knew this just from looking at you. Now that I'm here, I can see that as clearly as he could. I'm not going to stick around because my work is dangerous and could put you at risk. I will leave some money with your mother as well as my contact details. If ever either of you needs me, I'll be there to help in any way I can. Take care, young man, I get the feeling you and I have not seen the last of one another…'

To be continued…

Let me know what you think of this prequel
by leaving a review at e-store you purchased from
or by visiting my Facebook page:
https://www.facebook.com/SkyeCitySeries/

Thank you for reading
And have a great day!

Printed in Great Britain
by Amazon